# THE OMEGA'S

# Secret Baby

## OCEANPORT OMEGAS BOOK ONE

By
Ann-Katrin Byrde

**Cover Design** by Ana J. Phoenix

This is a work of fiction. Any similarity between the characters and situations within its pages and places or persons, living or dead, is unintentional and co-incidental.

This book contains sexually explicit scenes and adult language and may be considered offensive to some readers. Please don't read if you are under eighteen.

# DEDICATION

For Sherry Jones, who provided the name of the
baby in this book. And for all of my other wonderful
readers who encourage and enable me.

# Elias

---

*Please let today go smoothly.*

My seven-year old son bounced on the sidewalk beside me and our family dog, ten-year old Labrador Fiona. He was excited; I was anxious, and I gripped his hand tightly. It was his first day back at school after the winter holidays. Jake loved school, but he rarely got along with the other children. And just before the holidays, he'd gotten into a shouting match with one of the other kids that landed him in his first ever detention. It seemed he'd already forgotten all about that, but his alpha genes were starting to express themselves, and I worried that he was going to make a trend of it.

"Look, there's Tommy!" he said, pointing ahead where I could see little Tommy Fuller standing in front of the school gates with his father—another omega like me. Unlike me, though, Tommy Fuller's father wasn't a single dad.

I slowed down a bit even as Jake tried to pull me forward. "Hang on, sweetie," I said, making him

1

stop. I had no intention whatsoever of getting dragged into a conversation with another parent. I went down on one knee to be on eye-level with my son. He eyed me impatiently as I tried to straighten the wild locks of his blond hair. The same hair as his other father, but Jake didn't know that. It was better that way.

Or so I kept telling myself.

"Can I go now?" he asked, glancing at Tommy, who was waving at him.

"Okay, but remember what I told you."

"I know! No singing in class."

"Good boy." I pressed my lips to his forehead and Fiona put her nose to mine as if she thought it was time for a group-hug. Jake laughed and hugged the black dog—his favorite playmate.

I shook my head at the both of them. "Listen to your teacher, okay?"

"Okay."

"And play nice with the other children."

Jake looked at me with eyes so full of defiance it was difficult to believe he was only seven. "Only if they're nice to me too."

"They'll treat you the way you treat them," I tried to impart some wisdom to my little troublemaker.

He huffed.

I suppressed a sigh as I got to my feet again, knowing that any more parental advice would be lost on him just now. "Alright, you can go with Tommy. I'll be back later to get you."

He grinned. "Later, Daddy!"

"I love you," I called after him, but he was already running off, unafraid.

He'd never been a clingy kid. Considering that I'd always had to work to keep us fed, that was fortunate. And I had work to get to now as well, so I gently tugged on Fiona's leash and turned back the way we'd come. Internally I congratulated myself for having escaped a run-in with the other parents.

* * *

The day couldn't continue to go that smoothly of course. As soon as I got into work, I was swamped with things to do. Working at a small town's even smaller animal shelter wasn't what I'd always dreamed of doing, but it was still a job I enjoyed—and one that I knew I was lucky to have. Recently, though, things were becoming difficult. In short, the shelter struggled with financial issues. There was never enough money for all the things the animals needed. Food, vaccines, medications... We only had five dogs, four cats and two birds at the moment, but taking care of them wasn't cheap. And lately, one of my co-workers, an arrogant guy in his mid-thirties by the name of Harold, had gotten it into his head that one of us was going to be laid off—and it wasn't going to be him. No, it was going to be the omega, because who cared about omegas? They weren't made for the workplace anyway, right?

Harold took every opportunity he could get to dig into me. That day too, he went, "You're late!" as soon as I arrived at the shelter.

3

I ignored him as I unleashed Fiona and led her to the other dogs—one of the perks of working at the shelter—no one cared if I was bringing my own dog with me so long as she wasn't getting in the way. Most of my co-workers had adopted one or two animals in the time they'd worked here so this was nothing unusual.

"Hey, I'm talking to you," Harold insisted. He wasn't in a higher position than me at work; we were both really on the lowest rung of the ladder, but you wouldn't know it from his behavior.

"I heard you," I said, slowly turning to him. "But I'm not late." Well, maybe two minutes, but I couldn't take my son to school any earlier than I already did.

He shook his head. "You're always late. You know I'm not the only one who notices either." He nodded his head in the direction of the boss's office, as if trying to tell me that I needed to watch out.

I merely shrugged. "I'm doing the best I can." And considering that I was severely underpaid, that had to be enough. But underpaid or not, I couldn't afford to lose this job because my rude co-worker made me ignore my responsibilities, so I tried to cut the conversation with Harold short. "Excuse me, but I have a few dogs who need to be taken out on their morning walk. Don't want to make them wait any longer."

"They shouldn't have to wait at all," Harold called after me, but I ignored him. Who needed to talk to people like Harold when there were so many lovely dogs here? All five of them wagged their tails excitedly when they saw me enter the kennel with the leashes. They were used to their routine and knew exactly what was coming. And I think it wouldn't be too much to say that they liked me. I'd always been good with animals. Cats, dogs, birds, mice, it didn't matter. I could look into their eyes and establish some sort of immediate understanding. Or at least it felt like that to me. Doing anything like that with actual people was far harder. Humans were infinitely more complicated than animals.

"Are you all ready to go?" I asked the dogs. The smallest of them, a Yorkshire terrier who'd been with us for two months, stood up on her hind paws and yipped at me. I laughed. This wasn't the life I'd dreamed of, but it wasn't bad. I could forget my problems while I was with my furry friends— sadly though, that didn't mean they ceased to exist.

\* \* \*

It was just ten minutes before my lunch break when I heard the dreaded sound of my phone ringing. These days, that *never* meant good news. It was either going to be someone wanting money from me or Jake's school.

And with how things had been going with Jake lately, I found myself praying for the former.

I had no such luck, of course.

The familiar voice of the school's secretary greeted me when I picked up the phone.

"Mr. Stephens?"

I gulped, feeling almost like I was the one in

5

trouble rather than my kid. "Yes?"

"It'd be of great help if you could come down to the school. I'm afraid Jake's punched one of the other students."

I sighed. Jake was such a sweet kid when he was at home. Why could he never behave around other children? He wasn't stupid. In fact, all his teachers agreed with me that he was pretty smart. Just not smart enough to know how to handle social situations, it seemed.

"I'll be there as fast as I can," I said, glancing at my watch. If I was lucky, I could make it back before my lunch break was over.

"The other child's parents will be here as well," the secretary informed me.

I suppressed another sigh. It was bad enough being the single omega parent. It was even worse to be the single omega parent of a misbehaving child. Made everyone feel vindicated in their beliefs that omegas should not spend their lives unmated.

I ran a hand through my hair and ended the call. Nothing I could do about it now. This was how things were. Especially in a small town like Oceanport where everyone had their nose in everyone else's business.

Just the week before, my brother had informed me he'd heard that people down at the pub were making bets on who would finally manage to put a claim on me.

I shuddered, recalling that conversation. There weren't a lot of unmated alphas in town, and none of them appealed to me in the slightest.

And none of them would have been a good father for Jake.

There was only one man who could fill that role, and he... wasn't even aware of Jake's existence.

It was better that way. It was the choice I'd made after thinking about it long and hard all those years ago. I couldn't change it now.

Or so I thought.

Deciding to leave my dog at the shelter for the duration of the lunch break, I headed out to my car. Not, of course, without being scolded by Harold as I passed. "Coming late and leaving early?"

"Family emergency," I responded, biting back every comment I wanted to make about not coming early. Not that I'd seen a lot of action in the years since Jake had been born. Or rather, since Jake had been conceived.

"You always got some sort of emergency going on," he huffed.

I chose not to respond to that as I sat in my car, a beat up blue Ford, and pulled the door shut. The school wasn't a long way—nothing really was in Oceanport—but if I wanted to be back by the end of my lunch break, I had to get going now.

Pulling out of the shelter's parking lot, I went on my way.

It started snowing just as I drove onto the main road leading me back into the heart of the small town, big white flakes sailing onto the front screen of my car. Idly I wondered whether I'd thought to put a scarf on Jake this morning, and then whether he'd wear it. The boy often left his coats, scarves and mittens behind when he ran out to play, no matter how loudly I reprimanded him. I loved him fiercely, but he'd always had a mind of his own. I could only hope that it wasn't going to become too much of a problem for him. After all, I could remember a time when I hadn't listened to anyone else either, and that hadn't gone too well for me.

I reached Oceanport's elementary school after a short drive and got out of the car. At this point, I was already familiar with the way to the principal's office, so it didn't take me long to get there either.

As I had feared, the other child's mother was already there when the secretary led me into the office. I recognized the blond head of the kid my son had fought with instantly. Mike, or Miles, or something like that. Jake didn't like the boy, and he made no secret of it when he talked about school. I was reasonably sure the other boy's last name was Foster. His father ran the town's supermarket, and at the moment, his mother was regarding me with an air of disdain that was almost palpable. It was nothing new, although she usually hid her opinion of me a little bit better when we ran into each other during school events.

Ignoring her for now, I looked to the principal, Mr. Stein.

"What happened?"

"Your child is out of control, that's what happened!" Mrs. Foster screeched, even though she hadn't been asked.

"Please, Mrs. Foster," Mr. Stein cut her off.

"My baby has been hurt by this wild—"

"I'm very sorry for what happened to your child," I spoke up before she could insult Jake, although I wasn't overly pleased with my son myself that moment. "Please be assured that it won't happen again." I took a moment to glare at my offspring, who stubbornly looked at his feet instead of meeting my gaze.

Whatever was I going to do with him?

Before I could come to a decision, Mrs. Foster started screeching again. "You know this happens because he has no positive role model in his life!"

And this was exactly why I hated being around the other parents and their judgmental—

"Leave my daddy alone!" Jake spoke up, interrupting my thoughts. Everyone in the room turned to him. He met every questioning look with a challenging one. That was *not* going to get him out of trouble.

And I had no idea what to think about the fact that he felt like he had to protect me.

I just wanted to take him by the hand and leave this room.

"No one is trying to attack your dad, Jake," the headmaster said. "Please wait outside. You too, Miles."

Once the children were outside, I apologized for my son's behavior. "I don't know what's gotten into him."

"He'll be suspended for the rest of the day," the headmaster said, "but since this is his first violent offense, he can come back tomorrow. He'll be in detention for the rest of the week. And I hope nothing like this happens again. We do take these matters seriously."

"I understand. Now, if you could excuse me and Jake, I have to get back to work."

"Work." Mrs. Foster scoffed. "You'd better put some time into taming your child."

I gave her a tight-lipped smile because I could suddenly imagine just how *her* child had gotten himself punched. "I'll consider it," I said, leaving the office and taking my son with me as I headed back to the car.

Neither of us spoke on our way to the parking lot. It was only when we'd both climbed into the Honda that I trusted myself to start the conversation without raging at my son for being stupid.

"What do you have to say for yourself?"

Jake pressed his lips together and played with his seatbelt in the back of the car.

I took a deep breath. "Don't make me late for work. I'll put you in a cage with the birds." Jake didn't like the birds. He found them too loud.

"That's not fair!" he burst out.

"What's not fair is that I had to come all the way here because you *punched* another child! What's gotten into you? We don't punch people!" If I'd failed to teach him that, maybe Mrs. Foster was right and I was a horrible parent.

Jake pouted. "He was mean."

"I don't care how mean he was. People are mean to me all the time, and I don't—"

"That's why! People are mean to you and you don't do anything!"

I blinked as my son nearly screamed at me, his little hands balled into fists. "Jake..."

"He said I don't have another dad because you don't know who my other dad is, because you're a stupid omega."

His words felt like a punch to my vitals.

*Oh, Jake. I'm so sorry.*

I took a moment to close my eyes and regret every choice I'd ever made that led to my son defending my honor on the school yard. I didn't care what people said about me, but I hadn't given enough thought to how my reputation affected Jake. "You know it's not like that, right?" I asked softly, all my anger evaporating.

"That's why I punched him!"

I wished he sounded a *little* less proud. "You can't do it again. You have to promise me that." He could get thrown out of school for behavior like that, and what would I do with him?

"Only if he doesn't say it again."

"A lot of people say a lot of stupid things. But you still can't punch them. I'm going to be very upset if you do this again."

He looked at his shoes again.

"Jake," I prodded. "Will you promise me that you won't do this again?"

Finally, he nodded.

I released a breath and started the car, moderately sure that the worst part of the day was behind me.

11

I was wrong.

# Matthew

The roads were covered in snow by the time my driver reached Oceanport. I'd forgotten how bad the weather got around here this time of year. I hadn't come back to town often since I graduated school, and even when I was still a kid, I'd lived at boarding schools for the majority of the time.

In short, I didn't feel a major connection to Oceanport. It was a lovely town, presumably, with its quiet roads and its coastal charm, and it was certainly located in a scenic area, with a harbor on one side of the town and a mountain range stretching out into the distance on the other. It was nice to look at, but that was all it was. I felt no real connection to this place.

In fact, I hoped I didn't have to stay long. I'd come because I'd received some troubling news regarding my father's health.

And because I had some troubling news of my own to share.

When my parents' mansion came into view in

front of the car, I took a deep breath and counted to ten in my head.

My mother wasn't going to like what I was going to tell her, but I was an alpha, and too old to bow to her will. It had been eight years since I'd moved out on my own, for heaven's sake.

Still, it was going to be an unpleasant conversation.

I almost asked the driver to make a detour around town.

But it was time to face the music, so I got out of the car when it stopped and approached my family's house, which had never much felt like a home.

Three stories high, this mansion had been built to symbolize only one thing—my family's wealth. My parents were proud of this house, but to me it had only ever been a place I wanted to escape from.

I hadn't known, of course, that the outside world wasn't going to be any better.

"Sir, would you like me to carry your luggage inside?" the driver asked.

I nodded. "That would be very kind of you."

Approaching the front door, I didn't have to knock to see it opened. I wasn't surprised. No one could drive up here without being noticed.

A maid stood in the door, giving me a tight smile. I hadn't seen her before, but that wasn't surprising either. My mother went through staff like other people went through their underwear. "The Misses is expecting you in the sitting room.

14

Shall I take your coat?"

I took my coat off and handed it to her. "Thank you," I said, and then I went to face my mother.

My father wasn't with her when I entered the sitting room. That was unusual. Maybe it was true what my sister said and he really wasn't feeling well lately.

But I had no time to think about that any further when my mother came to greet me.

"Matthew, so good to have you back in town!" Her smile looked almost genuine, but not quite. So she already suspected that I hadn't come here just because.

"It's good to see you too, Mother."

She led me to one of the arm chairs. "Sit with me. Will you have tea or coffee?"

"Tea." I preferred coffee, really, but I had to watch my blood pressure. Or at least, my doctor suggested I do so, now that I was going to be an unmated alpha and all.

"Of course, dear." My mother related my request to the maid and sat. She already had a cup of coffee in front of her. She'd probably been waiting impatiently ever since I'd informed her of my visit. My mother was a lot of things, but she was not a patient woman. "What brings you here, darling?" she asked, seconds after the maid had left.

I leaned back in my chair. "Can't I simply visit my parents? I notice Father isn't with you tonight."

"He's resting." She waved her hand as if it was no big matter. "You know we would be delighted to see you more often, but we understand that you have a business to run."

Ah yes, the family business. "The business will survive my absence for a few days. My staff is excellent." And they were. I'd handpicked most of them to ensure I didn't have idiots working on my team. Idiots were bad for my blood pressure. My family owned a chain of hotels and coastal resorts. After I'd graduated school, I'd been put in charge of a hotel we'd recently bought from the competition, and I'd made it my own.

"Things are going well then?" my mother asked.

"Well enough," I said, and I couldn't go into further detail before the maid returned with tea for me. I took it and thanked her with a smile. She seemed surprised.

I set the cup of tea down on the table and looked at my mother. It was time to break the news to her and really get this visit started.

And she gave me the perfect jumping off point. Raising an eyebrow she said, "I can't help but notice your wife isn't with you."

I licked my lips. "Danielle is with her own family."

"And why is that? You're letting your wife travel on her own? That is not how I raised you."

"I'm not letting my wife travel on her own." It was difficult to keep from making a face. As if I'd ever *let* Danielle do anything. She'd always done what she wanted.

"Then explain to me why you're here and

she's not."

I folded my hands in my lap and looked into my mother's eyes. "Danielle is not my wife anymore."

Both of my mother's eyebrows went up, and then they came down again in a scowl. "What are you talking about?"

"We got a divorce." I kept my tone level, emotionless. My mother didn't need to know how I felt about this.

"A divorce!" My mother's voice went up a pitch. "Why would you do something so disgraceful? Are you trying to put your father in an early grave?"

Now it was on me to raise my eyebrows. "I wasn't aware that Father had health problems," I lied, because she probably didn't know that my sister and I had talked about this. And I really wanted to know how much truth there was to that. My sister had never been above manipulating people with made-up information. When we were kids, she'd convinced me my favorite brand of chocolate was poisonous to alphas so she could have it while I tried to empty the contents of my stomach in the toilet bowl. She was ruthless.

She made Mommy and Daddy proud.

"Don't try to distract from the topic," my mother scolded me. "We're talking about you now, not your father. How could you drive poor Danielle to divorce you? Did we raise you that poorly?"

Part of me wanted to point out that my parents had hardly spent any time raising me at all,

17

but I got the feeling it wasn't wise to enrage her further. No reason to make this trip even more unpleasant than it had to be. And I had to set the record straight. "Danielle didn't divorce me. I asked for the divorce."

One, two, three seconds of absolute silence, and then my mother exploded.

"How could you do that? She was perfect for you! I made sure that she was perfect for you! Don't you know how much time I've invested into finding you a spouse as good as her?"

*I don't need a spouse. I need a mate.*

I didn't voice that thought, but she must have seen something in my eyes. I'd never been good at keeping what I thought from showing on my face.

"What?" she snapped. "Were you not happy with her?" She shook her head. "Your father and I have always done our best to make sure you lacked for nothing, that you got the best education there was, that you got a suitable spouse... and yet you insist on being selfish. It wasn't good enough for you, was it?"

"I appreciate all you've done for me, but Danielle and I were too young." And the more time we spent together, the more we realized that we were not made for each other. We never connected. Danielle was a proud woman, and every bit as entrenched in higher society as my mother was. She would never have asked for a divorce, but I knew that she got no joy out of our marriage.

"Too young." My mother scoffed. "You're still too young. You don't know what's good for you."

I gave her a wry smile. "I'm nearly thirty, Mother."

"*Nearly* thirty." My mother made an unamused sound, then she rested her head in her hands as if devastated. "You can't live out there as a young and rich unmated alpha. They're going to come at you like a pack of hungry harpies." Her shoulders heaved.

I thought she was laying on the drama a bit thick, but I wasn't completely unsympathetic. She truly believed all she was saying. There had been a time in my life when I'd believed it myself—that I needed to be married to lead a respectable life, that every omega I ever met would only be interested in my body and my money...

I wasn't so sure anymore. Every time I tried to remind myself that I shouldn't look at other men, the image of one particular omega sprang to mind.

*Elias.*

Elias hadn't cared about my money.

He'd certainly tempted me to abandon my virtues, though. So maybe there was *some* truth to what my mother was saying.

"I'll be careful, Mother," I tried to console her, putting my hand on her arm.

She was having none of it and slapped my hand away as if it was dirty. "Is that why you don't have children? Because you were planning on sabotaging this marriage from the start?"

Sabotage my marriage? "I've done no such thing. We weren't in love. You can't force these things." I knew, because I'd certainly tried.

"You have duties to this family!" My mother stopped the fake sobbing to glare at me instead. "If you won't go back to Danielle, we'll find you another woman to add children to this family, but don't think I'll let you sully our name by living like a bachelor and inviting lusty omegas into your bed."

"I think I'd rather not jump straight into another marriage."

I don't know why I even bothered saying that because nothing could stop my mother when she got like this. She was on a roll now; her opinions and feelings were facts, and there wasn't anything anyone could say to convince her differently.

"I'm not letting you off the hook so easily," she said. "First thing tomorrow I'm going to call poor Danielle to see if this can't be fixed. You can't give up so easily, Matthew. That is not how your father and I raised you."

Right. "Do what you must, Mother." I got up from the chair. "I'm going to go for a walk."

For a moment, she looked like she was going to stop me, but then she only sighed and waved her hand at me to go. "Be careful," she said. "There's ice on the roads. Don't slip and break your neck. I don't want you in a cast during your next wedding."

My mother had always had an odd way of showing she cared.

I knew that she *did*, in her own way, but I still couldn't wait to get out of this town again. There wasn't anything worth staying for, after all.

Or so I'd thought.

# Elias

I was exhausted by the time I made it home that evening. Since I'd had to drop Jake home before returning to work earlier, I'd been a bit later in getting back to the shelter than I'd hoped. Harold hadn't let me hear the end of it all day. Still, I knew I was lucky I even had the option of letting Jake stay home instead of taking him to work with me. That only worked because I was living with my brother.

"Thank God you're home," Griff greeted me almost as soon as I opened the door and Fiona charged ahead inside the house. "You can entertain your hellion now. I have work to do."

"I'm sorry. Was he a lot of trouble?" I bit my lips, hating that I had to inconvenience my brother like this. He'd done all he could to help me and Jake since my son's birth, and it was perfect that he had a job that allowed him to work from home, but I knew that I shouldn't abuse that fact.

"He was good," Griff said. "But you know I

can't focus on my work when he's watching cartoons."

"Only because you want to watch cartoons too."

He smiled and scratched the back of his head. "Busted." His expression turned serious again. "Tell me though, what did this other kid do that Jake decided to punch him? He wouldn't tell me."

I stepped around my brother and went into our small kitchen. "Where is he now?"

Griff pointed at the couch just across from the kitchen island where I found my son fast asleep, clutching one of the throw pillows. "I already took a picture."

"Of course you did." Griff's amusement made me smile. He was a photographer and a graphic designer. He did fantastic work, producing stunning images. If you paid him to do it. Left to his own devices, all he wanted to do was take goofy snapshots of his friends and family.

I grabbed myself a cup of coffee and sat down with it at the kitchen island. The coffee had probably been made a while ago as it was only lukewarm, but I didn't mind.

"So what happened?" Griff asked in a hushed tone.

I sipped at my coffee just to get a second to think about how I was going to word my response. "Apparently the rumors flying around about me have made it to the playground."

Griff winced. "Ouch. Kids can be cruel."

I shook my head. "They're just parroting what

they hear from their parents. I told Jake he can't punch anyone, but honestly... "

"Kind of makes you want to, doesn't it?"

"Yeah." I drank some more of the coffee. "And then of course I got back to work late and had to listen to Harold's shit all day."

"You really need to quit that job."

"The job's not so bad, the coworkers..." I let the sentence hang.

Griff gave me a grim smile and I knew what he was going to say before he opened his mouth. "You could do so much better than being the designated boy for everything at the local shelter."

"Not without a degree I can't," I reminded him, only half my attention on the conversation because I'd heard it all before. My brother *loved* to remind me of all that I could have been in another life. If I wasn't an omega. Or maybe it wasn't just that I was an omega.

Griff was an omega too.

But he hadn't fucked up the way I had.

It was a little bit humiliating to be berated by my baby brother.

"I know you've been thinking about going back to school," Griff said.

I raised an eyebrow at him. I'd entertained the thought yes, but I hadn't discussed it with him. Mostly because I'd dismissed the idea.

"I saw a page about vet school opened on your laptop the other day," Griff explained. "You could still do it."

"I have enough on my plate with my job at the

23

shelter and Jake. I don't need to be a vet."

"I can watch Jake while you're studying."

I set the mug down with a sigh. I appreciated the offer but... "Jake's my responsibility. I don't want to keep holding you back." My little brother had already done enough for me. It was time he got out of this house a little and started living his own life. I was sure there was a good mate somewhere out there for him, if only he took the time to look.

"You're not holding me back." Griff's expression turned the slightest bit sad. "I used to look up to you, you know."

*Used to.* Ow. He probably hadn't meant for his words to come out that way, but they hurt.

"You showed me that omegas could get scholarships if they tried hard enough," he went on. "I can't stand to see you let yourself be kicked around by the fu... by the freaking gossips in this town! You have to—"Griff stopped himself when he was interrupted by my son climbing on the stool next to him.

Neither of us had noticed Jake get up, but he was looking at us curiously now.

"Are you fighting?"

"No, we're not fighting," I said. "Actually I was just about to take Fiona out for a walk." She probably didn't need it, but I did.

"I'm coming!" Jake decided.

I wanted to say no and have some time for myself, but Jake was already running off to fetch the leash, an excited dog at his heels. The image made me smile. Especially when Jake put Fiona's

24

blue woolen hat on her. She looked so silly with that thing on, but Jake loved it.

And I had to admit that no, not everything in my life was bad. I had the best kid and the best dog, and that made up for a lot.

"Okay, you can come," I told my son. "But no throwing snow balls at the dog."

Jake considered this for a moment. "Can I throw snow balls at you?"

"Don't you *dare*."

He only grinned.

\* \* \*

Our walk took us a little farther out than usual, to the park where I'd first found Fiona when she was still a stray. I wasn't really surprised that my feet led me to this place. I often found myself coming here when I was feeling nostalgic. It was a nice park. High trees, wide patches of green, lots of benches to sit on and a swing set for children.

Roughly nine years ago, I'd met Jake's *other* father here for the first time.

I'd been home from college on my first summer break, trying to read a book in the shade of the large oak at the outskirts of the park where it was quiet, when I'd heard the playful yips of a puppy. When I'd gone to investigate, I'd found a guy my age play-fighting with a young black dog behind the bushes.

I'd never talked to the guy before, but I recognized him anyway. He was Matthew Lowell. In a town the size of Oceanport, you knew who the wealthiest bachelor was, even if you weren't looking to get hitched. Everybody knew of the Lowells. If the rumors were true, they had more money than the rest of the town combined, and that kind of wealth sparked interest everywhere.

Once I knew who I was intruding on, I took a step back, but it was too late. Matthew had already turned his eyes on me. Warm brown eyes.

I'd never dated before, never even been tempted, so I wasn't sure what to make of that tingling sensation I felt in my gut when this handsome stranger smiled at me.

I should have run.

I knew that now, but I didn't know it back then.

And I was ripped out of my reverie when my son hit me in the face with a snowball.

"You little...!" I growled, wiping the snow off.

Jake held his belly laughing. "Your face! I got you!"

"Wait, you!" I bent down to scoop some snow up in my hands and throw it at him.

He ran, still laughing.

"You can't escape!" I gave chase, dog barking at my side as we plowed through the snow.

"Catch me, Daddy!" Jake yelled back at me, not looking where he was going until he ran head-first into a man coming down the road from the other direction. I could do nothing but watch him knock the stranger over until the both of them landed in a heap on the cold ground.

I ran up to them. "Are you alright?" I peeled

my kid off the other man. "I'm so sorry. We were playing and he wasn't looking," I apologized, patting the snow off Jake.

"I'm sorry," Jake apologized as well.

I looked back at the stranger only to feel even more embarrassment as I saw my dog lick his face. At least he seemed to take it in stride. Actually, he was taking it far too well, hugging my excited dog like an old friend and whispering her name with a sense of wonder.

"Fiona..." he said, as if he couldn't believe what he was seeing.

And I couldn't believe what I was hearing.

Who was this guy?

I squinted, heart racing.

Could it be?

One drawback of this park was how poorly illuminated it was during the evening hours, but...

I crouched down to take my dog from the stranger, and one whiff of the other man's intoxicating scent told me all I needed to know; he was an alpha. One that I knew intimately.

*Matthew.*

# Matthew

All I'd wanted when I'd left the mansion was to get some fresh air. I'd never thought I'd run into Fiona again—and in this park too! There was no mistaking her, though. This was the same crazy black dog who'd caught my attention years ago, on another day that I'd desperately needed to escape from my parents.

The day I'd met Elias.

Who had eventually gone on to adopt Fiona. I remembered that much.

Which meant...

If Fiona was here...

I looked at the kid who'd run me over, then at the man crouching next to me. What were the odds I would run into Elias my first day back home out here in the park?

"This really is a small town," I found myself mumbling, staring at him.

He blinked, and then he laughed. There wasn't a lot of light, but I could just make out that he still had those adorable dimples that had attracted me to him all those years ago. Aside from his scent, anyway. All omegas had a certain scent to them that could drive an alpha crazy in the right situation, but Eli's seemed even stronger than usual, at least to me. Eli was special. I'd known that from the moment I'd seen him in the park, with a book in his hands and a curious light in his eyes that seemed to shine even brighter when he looked at the dog.

And now he stood in front of me again, unexpected.

"I didn't know you were in town," he muttered. He straightened, and for a moment it appeared as if he wanted to offer me a hand, but then he didn't.

*Shying away from touch?*

I got up on my own and brushed the snow off myself. "You couldn't know. I only just arrived. I know rumors fly fast in this town, but I guess not as fast as your little guy here." I glanced at the kid who'd barreled into me, wondering if he was Eli's. It occurred to me that I'd know if I'd kept up with the town's gossip, but that had never appealed to me. Not when I was so often in the center of it.

And it didn't surprise me to see Eli with a child—he was an omega after all, but the sight still made my chest constrict. I just hoped whoever had fathered the boy was treating him right.

"I'm sorry," Eli said, taking another step away from me and pulling the child toward himself. "He can be a bit wild."

"He's an alpha," I said, because the scent lay in the air, even though it was weak.

"I know," Eli said quietly, an apprehensive look

29

on his face. Something was wrong. I just couldn't quite put my finger on it.

"Daddy, who is that man?" the boy finally spoke up, voice full of curiosity at the same time as he glared at me, as if he'd decided that, whoever I was, he needed to protect his Daddy from this strange man in front of him.

He was a little alpha all right. One who showed early, too. Most children took until their teenage years to display any alpha or omega tendencies.

"This is Matthew Lowell," Eli introduced me, matter-of-factly. "You know that big house at the top of the hill that we see when we go sledding? That's where his family lives."

"Ooooh. Can he sled on the big hill?"

I laughed. "I haven't gone sledding in a long time. But my sister and I have taken our sleds up there when we were children."

This earned me another, "Ooooh," while I could see his Daddy grow visibly more uncomfortable with every passing second. Had he mated one of those ridiculously possessive alphas who didn't want their mates to talk to other alphas or what was going on here?

I'd thought we'd parted on amicable terms, all things considered. I could still remember that last night. We'd certainly made it count. Part of me still wished it hadn't been our *last* night, but all good things had to come to an end, and we'd been good. *Really* good. I could still remember the way Eli felt underneath me, around me, all warm and tight and...

And I had to shove those thoughts aside if I

didn't want my hormones to spin out of control. There was no point in getting worked up over a mated omega. Thing was, though, he still smelled as if he was unmated. Available. And that smell tugged on all my alpha instincts that wanted to have him.

I took a deep breath, and that didn't make it better.

I had to distract myself, so I focused my attention on the child. "Do you like to go sledding?" I asked.

"I love it!" he exclaimed, and his honest enthusiasm made me chuckle.

"Cute kid," I told Eli. "How old is he?"

Eli bit his lower lip. For some reason, the question seemed to make him even more uncomfortable than he already was.

"I'm seven!" the child announced proudly. "I'm in second grade already."

"Really?" I'd expected him to be a little younger. If this kid was seven already, Eli must have gotten himself pregnant very quickly after I'd left, and I wasn't sure what to think of that. Not that I had any right to think *anything* of that. I'd gotten married, after all.

It didn't matter that I'd still secretly thought of Eli on my wedding night.

"It was very nice seeing you, Matt," Eli said. "But we have to go home now. It's nearly Jake's bed time."

So his name was Jake, huh?

"I don't want to go to bed yet," Jake protested. "What about our snowball fight?"

"Only boys who behave in school get to stay up longer."

"I'll be good!"

"Good," Eli said, taking his son's small hand in his own. "Then we can have a snowball fight tomorrow."

Jake eyed him suspiciously. "Promise?"

"Promise."

Jake huffed, but didn't say anymore after that.

"We'll be on our way." Eli looked at me. "You probably shouldn't stay out too long either," he advised me in a soft tone and I couldn't help but feel reminded of the time we'd hidden away in one of my parents' cabins in the woods and he'd used this same tone of voice to remind me that 'we probably shouldn't be here.' But he'd surrendered just as soon as I'd run my hand into his soft hair and touched my lips to his.

The memory sent a shiver down my spine. I'd never felt as strongly about anyone as I felt about this omega. But I couldn't hang on to that. I'd left him, and he was a mated man now, even if my senses didn't want to believe it.

"Goodbye, Eli. Jake."

"Goodbye, Matt."

"Bye, Matt!" Jake echoed.

Fiona sniffed on my leg. I crouched to pet her head. "Goodbye, old girl."

Eli had to tug on her leash to get her away from me, and it was like he tugged on my heartstrings at the same time. A part of me wanted to jump up and stop Eli from leaving, but that was ridiculous. What

more could I say to him?
        Nothing.

# Elias

I went down into the living room after I'd tucked Jake in bed and found my brother sitting on the couch with his laptop. He was probably busy with some sort of work, but I couldn't worry about that now. I needed to talk to someone. And since Griff was the only one I'd ever told about Matt, he was the only one I could talk *to*.

"Matthew Lowell is back in town," I announced, grabbing his attention. He turned away from the laptop's screen and looked at me.

"I hadn't heard."

"Me neither." I chewed my bottom lip. A nervous habit I'd *thought* I'd quit. Apparently not. "I ran into him in the park. Well, actually, Jake ran into him. Literally."

Griff raised an eyebrow at me. I couldn't blame him. My life was officially weird. "You mean you met him while you were out on your walk?"

"Yes!"

Griff put the laptop aside now. "Tell me

more."

"We went to the park. Jake was running ahead and not looking, and literally ran into him. I didn't know who he was at first, so I scrambled to apologize and all and then... Well, I got a whiff of him." I sighed. "Can you believe he still smells the same?"

Griff laughed. Of course he did. I sounded like a teen omega in heat.

*Calm down, Eli. No point in getting worked up over this.*

I'd abandoned the idea of getting back together with Matt years ago, before Jake had even been born, and Jake was who I needed to think of now. Obviously.

So far, staying away from Matt had been easy because he'd only visited this town a few times after moving away and never for long. He'd never met Jake before.

"So he's met Jake?" Griff asked, as if reading my thoughts.

"Yeah." I looked toward the hallway, a little paranoid that my son might climb out of bed again and listen in to our conversation, but he was usually a good sleeper.

"Do you think he's caught on? Jake does resemble him."

"Just his nose and his hair." And I kept his hair short for a reason, although it pained me to see his beautiful curls cut down. But there were already enough rumors flying around, and I didn't want any of our neighbors to draw a connection between

Jake and Matt.

"And his alpha genes," Griff added.

I nodded. "And that. But there's a lot of alphas." I ran a hand through my hair. "Jake told him how old he was, though."

Griff made a face. "Think Matt's going to put two and two together?"

I sighed. "He might. Either that or he's going to think I moved on very quickly." Even the idea felt jarring when the truth was that I'd *never* really moved on. I had become busy though, which had helped me not think of him and all the what-ifs.

"It could have happened, though," Griff pointed out. "A lot of omegas get mated quickly. You know not all of us get a say in it..."

"I know..." Griff and I were lucky our family was somewhat progressive. Not progressive enough not to throw me out, but still. A lot of people still believed it was best to have omegas mate as quickly as possible, to save us from ourselves and our 'uncontrollable urges', when it was really the alphas who claimed they couldn't control themselves around unmated omegas.

It was ridiculous, but it was difficult to change people's views.

I was glad my kid was not an omega. He was going to have an easier life as an alpha.

Griff nudged my shoulder. "I know I've asked this before, but... Honestly, do you ever regret not telling Matt?"

I let myself sink into the cheap leather of the couch. "You know he was already married when I found out."

"Yeah, but still..."

I closed my eyes and inhaled, because we'd already talked about this a million times and Griff would never get it. Still, my brother deserved my patience because he'd never said a word to our parents or anyone else, never let anything slip. I don't know what I would have done without him.

"His family would disown him," I explained for what felt like the hundredth time. The Lowell family definitely counted among the people with the most old-fashioned beliefs. To this day it still surprised me that their son had turned out be a decent human being.

"You had to make sacrifices too. It's not fair that he got to go on with his life while you had to drop everything. You shouldn't have had to do everything on your own."

"I didn't, though, did I?" I cocked my head at my brother. "I had you. And now I have an amazing son on top of it all. He's the one missing out, really."

Griff was quiet for a moment. Then he asked, "And do you think he's going to be pissed at you when he finds out?"

I grimaced. "Possibly."

"Maybe he'll just leave town again tomorrow," my brother mused. "Best case scenario, right?"

Was it, though? The more I thought about it, the less sure I became about what I wanted. Did I want Matt to find out about Jake? The possibility that he would be mad at me really was high, but the thought had occurred to me that Jake needed an alpha role model in his life. Someone who could stop him acting out the way he did.

But I had no guarantee that Matt would want to be that someone even if I told him that he was Jake's father. With that family of his, he'd probably assume all I wanted was money, and I couldn't stand that thought.

"Yeah," I said to Griff. "Let's just hope he leaves again. He's good at that, after all." And my life didn't need another complication. *Jake's* life didn't need another complication. We were happy with the way things were.

Weren't we?

# Matthew

"Matthew, are you listening?"

I looked up at Frederica with what was no doubt a guilty expression on my face. I hadn't been listening. I'd asked Frederica to have tea with me so I could hear her out about my father, but ever since the events of the night before, my attention had been drifting.

"You haven't heard a word, have you?" Frederica wagged her finger at me, something she'd been doing since I was a young boy. I had no idea how she'd survived in my family's service for so long when most of our other staff changed every year, but somehow, nobody dared to kick Frederica out, no matter what she did.

Which made her an invaluable source of information.

Frederica had her ears everywhere and knew everything.

About the town, my family, the rest of the staff...

I wouldn't have been surprised if the only

reason my mother didn't kick her out was because she was afraid what this maid might tell the townsfolk if she ever let her go. This lady was sure to have some blackmail material.

I didn't mind, though. Frederica had always been good to me. Even when she was scolding me—which actually used to happen quite a lot. "I'm sorry," I said, giving her all my attention. "What were you saying?"

"About your father." She took a sip of her tea. Green tea with milk. She was the only person I knew who drank it like that. "He hasn't been doing so well lately."

"That's in line with what my sister told me. But do you think it's something serious or that he's just getting on in age?"

She shook her head. "There have been doctor visits. Your parents say it's nothing, but the secrecy around it all makes me suspect there's more going on. Your sister might have heard something. The young lady is over every Sunday. And she's still every bit as pleasant as she used to be," she added in a low voice.

I couldn't help the laugh that bubbled up in me. My sister had never been pleasant. But perhaps this one time she hadn't lied. And I wasn't sure how to feel about this news. My father and I had never been close. I'd spent too much time away from home growing up, while he'd spent too much time working. But he was still my father.

"I'm sorry my sister is giving you trouble," I said to Frederica before I drank some of my own tea—with no milk in it.

She made a dismissive gesture with her hand. "She's no trouble. I know how to deal with her. I only wish I didn't have to clean up after her son. Now that kid is a *brat.*" She said it with a level of emphasis that made me chuckle again. My nephew was certainly not a well-behaved child. Every time I met the boy, I left feeling glad that I didn't have any children of my own.

Not that Danielle and I hadn't *tried.* It simply hadn't happened. One more thing that had put a strain on our marriage—and on my relationship with my mother. Still, the way things had ended, it was for the best.

"Promise me that you will not let your children torture me when you have some," Frederica said.

"I promise," I said easily, although I didn't want to think too much about children now. When I did, I couldn't help but think of Eli and his son. His seven-year old son. "Say, Frederica, how much do you know about what goes on in town these days?" It was a long shot, but maybe...

She raised an eyebrow at me. "You want to hear gossip?"

"Not *gossip*, no, but—"

"Oh, I didn't think I'd get to see the day you admit an interest in gossip." She seemed delighted now. "The stories I could tell you!"

I grimaced, and stopped her before she could tell me about the baker's son sleeping with the farmer's daughter in the parking lot of the movie

41

theater or whatever. "I was only wondering if you'd heard anything about an omega by the name of Elias Stevens."

Her eyes sparkled. "You like that omega?"

"He's an old friend," I waved her off.

"Is he the boy you made out with when you were young?"

I did a double take. What had she just said?

"Oh, don't think I didn't notice you sneaking into the house with this dreamy expression on your face. I know that wasn't because of your fiancé."

Ow, she was even more perceptive than I gave her credit for. No wonder she knew everything about everyone. I just hadn't thought that included *me*.

And I didn't know what to say now.

"Don't worry, dear," she said, a smile on her lips as she took another sip of her tea. "I never said a word to anyone. After all, you were always my favorite child. I can say that because I'm not your mother."

"Thank you." It was all that I could think to say in response.

She simply gave me another smile. "It's good to know that I was right and you had some fun before you got married. And with an omega too!"

I felt the tiniest bit of heat creep into my cheeks, because I'd definitely had *fun*, and Frederica was not someone I wanted to discuss my sex life with. She said she wasn't my mother, but honestly, some days it felt like she was.

"So you want to know how your past lover is

doing, yes? That's understandable. I still look in on my exes from time to time. Always interesting. Well, except for the one guy who gave me lice. I won't go anywhere near *that one* again." She said it with so much disdain in her voice that I had to grin, forgetting the awkwardness I'd felt a moment ago.

"If you know anything about Eli, I'd be glad to hear it."

"Eli, huh?" She set her tea down and thought for a moment. "I've heard about an omega with that name. He stands out, really, because he's old for being unmated."

"Unmated?" I repeated because I couldn't believe it. So my senses hadn't tried to trick me the night before. Eli really *was* still on the market. After all this time... I'd never have thought it possible. How lucky was I? All this time I'd dreaded finding out what lucky bastard had mated Eli, only to hear he was still single. *Available.*

*But not necessarily available to you.*

"Well, yes. He turns everyone down. Upsets some of the alphas in town. He's good-looking after all, but you know that." She winked at me. This topic obviously amused her. "To think that you of all people slept with him..."

"What's that supposed to mean?" I demanded.

"Nothing. Just that you're not exactly the type to go downtown and seduce the local omegas."

I shrugged. "It was a chance encounter."

She nodded. "Must have been. And the chemistry was right?"

"I'm not going into detail on that," I said, clearing my throat. Frederica didn't need to know about the way my heart had started racing the moment I'd seen Eli smile at me in the park all those years ago.

"Fine." Frederica waved her hand. "Be coy, then." She took her tea cup up again, her face turning pensive. "There's also the matter of the child, of course," she said after a minute.

"The child?" Holy shit, I'd nearly forgotten about Jake upon hearing that Eli was unmated.

"Eli's child. He has a young boy. No one knows who fathered him, though. It's a mystery. If you believe the rumors, he doesn't know himself."

I did *not* believe the rumors. "He's not that kind of person," I said quietly, processing all that Frederica had told me and coming to a realization. "He knows. I'm sure of it." Eli wasn't the type to sleep with random strangers, let alone multiple strangers. The chemistry between us had been out of control from the moment we'd met, but it had still taken me weeks to get him to drop his clothes for me. I'd had to work my way up from stolen kisses to tongue-on-tongue action to mindless make-out sessions in the dark. All of it had been worth it, though. *So* worth it.

"Well, if he knows, he's not telling anyone. People assume he was knocked up by some college kid, since he came home from school pregnant, and then he quit school soon after."

It saddened me to hear that. He'd only just started school when I'd met him, and he'd been so proud of that too. Getting that scholarship. He'd worked his ass off. That's why he told me he deserved to have a little fun. I couldn't believe that he let some college guy take that away from him. That simply couldn't be what had happened. Not to Eli. "His son is seven," I said, more to myself than to Frederica, who gave me a blank look in response.

"Is he?" she asked, but I wasn't really listening to her, stuck in my own head.

"I slept with him eight years ago."

Now Frederica was starting to catch on. "Oh." She held a hand in front of her mouth. "But then... do you think...?"

Did I? "I don't know." If Jake was really mine, Eli would have told me, wouldn't he?

Or, he wouldn't have told *anyone*.

My head was spinning.

Could it really be....?

No, I was jumping to conclusions.

"Oh, that would be *so* good if it was true." Frederica's eyes sparkled again.

*Oh no.* "Not a word!" I told her. "Not to anyone!" We couldn't have this kind of rumor floating around. People would be all over it, no matter if it was true or not. Knowing that I'd been together with Eli eight years ago would be proof enough for a lot of the people in this town. And I needed to process this information by myself before I wanted anyone else talking about it. If it was even true.

Frederica sighed. "I understand. But this is such big news. You could be a father!"

I felt the blood drain from my face because I was *not* ready to suddenly be the father of a seven-year old. "If Eli wanted me in his life, he would have told me." I rubbed my temples with the heels of my hands.

I had to speak to Eli again, and soon. Just so I could stop worrying about all of this, since it would certainly turn out to not be true. It had to. "I guess I'll be staying in town for a few days," I told Frederica.

"Lovely," Frederica said. "I'd thought you'd only stay the weekend."

"Well, I've got some things to look into, don't I?" Never mind that staying longer would also allow me to keep an eye on my father's health. "Would you happen to know where Eli lives? Or where he works?"

Frederica shrugged. "I don't know. But I can ask around."

"Thank you." I drained the rest of my tea and leaned back in my chair, feeling a migraine coming on.

The sooner this was all sorted the better.

# Elias

When I got into work the next day, it didn't seem like things were going to pick up for me. Because of the shelter's financial problems, my boss suggested that we do some sort of charity event to raise public awareness and get some donations coming in. It was a good idea, but my boss wasn't good at actually *planning* anything, so he proposed that Harold and I think of something. Together. Because that was totally how I wanted to spend my day.

For the better part of an hour, Harold and I stared at each other in silence, a blank page on the table in front of us.

"You're an omega," he said eventually.

"Yes..." I had no idea where he was going with this, but it couldn't be good.

"Couldn't we have like an auction? Put you to good use for once. I'm sure some people would pay money for a night with you."

My jaw dropped.

*Excuse me?*

"Are you suggesting I prostitute myself?" There was a line, and Harold had just pissed on it.

"I wasn't saying that," he claimed. "I meant like a date. Not my fault you immediately jump to sex, but I guess that's omegas for you."

*How dare he...*

Wordlessly, I stood and left the room. I was so mad I couldn't even think straight. All I knew was I needed to get out of there before I did something I might regret.

I only stopped when I reached the shelter's parking lot, still seething inside.

*That absolute bastard.*

I didn't want to skip out of work, but I did need some fresh air to cool off. Where did people get off, saying things like that? I wasn't sex-obsessed. In fact, I couldn't even remember the last time I'd gone to bed with anyone beyond the fact that it had been an entirely disappointing experience. That hadn't been the fault of my partner, though. After I knew what it felt like to have an actual connection with someone, nothing else could compare.

I was yanked out of my silent raging when I heard a car door open. Someone else beside me was in the parking lot. A customer maybe? I looked to the direction of the sound—only to see the man I'd been thinking of a mere second ago.

What was Matthew doing here? Did he know I worked here? I couldn't imagine that he'd come here because he wanted to adopt a puppy.

I folded my hands in front of my chest, and

not only because it was cold—which it was, more so because I'd stormed out without my coat.

"What brings you here?" I addressed Matt, trying not to let it show that I was having a bad day.

"I need to talk to you."

"So you waited for me in the parking lot?"

"I was going to go in." He shook his head. "I got a migraine."

"Oh. I'm sorry." He'd gotten those every now and then when we were younger too. I'd hated seeing him in pain, but sometimes, I could take it away. I wasn't quite sure how I did it myself, but he told me he found my presence soothing. 'That omega thing you do helps me,' he'd said, although I was never aware of doing anything special. I simply held him and massaged the back of his head with my fingers. What anyone would do, really. "Are you feeling better?" I asked, because I was tempted to go to him even now, my anger over Harold's stupid comment all but forgotten.

"I'm fine, thank you," he said. I wasn't sure that I believed him, but he changed the topic on me. "Are you off work now?"

"No, actually, I should probably go back in." I glanced at the entrance to the shelter behind me and rubbed my arms. I *really* should go back in.

Matt took a step toward me and shrugged out of his coat. "I understand. I'm not going to keep you long, but we do need to talk." And then he draped his coat over my shoulders without even asking me whether I wanted it—and in doing so, he came so close to me that the alpha scent he gave off nearly overwhelmed me. It was like I hadn't aged at all and I was still that stupid college freshman who'd fallen for him in the first place.

"What is it that you want to talk about?" I made myself ask, focusing on the present.

He looked around the parking lot. "I'm not sure we should do this here. How would you feel about having dinner with me tonight?"

I grimaced. "Do you want Jake to be there? Because I can't just leave my kid alone for a night."

"You can't find anyone to watch him for an hour or two?"

I licked my lips. "I *might* find someone, but where would you want to have dinner?" Matt had never taken me out to dinner. At least not in public. He'd sometimes ordered meals from fancy restaurants and we'd eaten them somewhere in a safe place, in a cabin in the woods or on one of his family's boats that never got any use. We'd gotten good at hiding away from the eyes of the town.

"Wherever you want," he offered.

I raised an eyebrow at him. "That's easy for you to say since you won't have to live with the rumors that'll be flying around after." No, he'd just leave again. And I shouldn't have dinner with him in the first place. Nothing good could come of it.

It didn't matter that he was everything I wanted.

Not when I knew that I couldn't have him.

I'd been naive eight years ago, thinking I could enjoy my time with him while it lasted and then move on as if nothing had happened. I hadn't known how much leaving him would *hurt*.

"Okay," Matt said. "No dinner then. What do you suggest?"

I thought about it for a moment. Part of me was tempted to simply deny him outright, but then I did want to know what he had to discuss with me. "I walk my dog every night at nine," I said. "I don't always go to the park, but sometimes I do."

"Got it." Matt gave me a small smile. "Thank you."

"You're welcome," I said, sighing, because I hated the way a simple smile from him *still* managed to make me feel warm even while I was positively freezing.

I could only hope that he left town again before I got any really stupid ideas.

# Matthew

I had no idea whether Eli was really going to show up, but I hoped he would—and not only because it was freezing out here tonight. I also hoped he was bringing his own coat this time, because I'd hate to part with mine again, although I would. Nothing made me more uncomfortable than seeing Eli uncomfortable. Especially when there was something I could do about it. I hadn't even thought about putting my coat on him earlier, as if we were still an item. It had just felt like the right thing to do.

And getting so close to him, I'd almost leaned in for a kiss too.

*Stupid.*

Just because Eli wasn't mated didn't mean he was available, or willing to start anything with me again. And I still had duties to my family, even if I didn't like them.

I rubbed my hands together and looked at the swing set across from me. I hadn't come to this park very often as a child. Mostly, I'd been confined to our property. And then when I'd finally ventured out into the world, I'd done exactly what my mother had always warned me of—I'd fallen for the first omega I'd met.

Not because he was the first, though.

No, because he was *Eli*. With his bright eyes and his kind smile and all his fierce ambitions that defied everything I'd been taught about omegas.

And I couldn't help but wonder what had happened to him after we'd parted. How had he turned into a source of gossip?

I exhaled and watched the air puff out of my mouth like smoke. It was ten past nine.

Was he really coming?

Well, if he was, I would be here waiting.

I stuck my hands into my pockets to keep them warm.

It took a couple more minutes until I saw someone approach under the park lights in the distance. Someone with a dog.

I smiled, and walked toward Eli.

"I'm sorry," he said in greeting. "I got held up by a boy who wanted to show me every page of his new comic book."

"It's fine," I said while Fiona happily sniffed my leg. "I'm just happy you could make it at all. I was beginning to worry."

"It was a pretty thick comic book."

I had to chuckle. "The woes of a parent, I assume. Should we walk a bit?"

"Yeah, let's. We'll get cold if we don't."

I licked my lips to keep from speaking, because part of me wanted to offer him some help *warming up*.

"What is it that you wanted to talk about?" He asked, cutting right to the chase once we'd walked a few feet.

"Well," I started. "It's been a while since we've seen each other."

He gave a short laugh that sounded anything but amused. "You could say that."

"I was wondering how you've been doing."

"I'm a single parent and I work at the shelter. I live with my brother. There's really not much more to say." And by his tone of voice, he didn't seem *inclined* to say more either.

"Forgive me for saying this, but you don't seem happy." He couldn't be. Not if I knew him at all. And I liked to think that I'd gotten to know him pretty well in the time we'd spent together. We'd only had a few months, but they'd been the most intense months of my life.

He gave me a wry smile. "I'm a parent. *My* happiness is not what concerns me the most. But you don't have to worry about me. I mean, it's kind of sweet that you do, but I'm fine."

"I guess I have no choice but to believe you." I took a deep breath, inhaling the night air, the smell of snow, and Eli's scent—which took me right back to a younger, bolder version of myself. "What would you do if I kissed you right now?"

Eli stopped and looked at me wide-eyed. "Are you serious? You show up here after eight years and suddenly you want to kiss me?"

The way he said it made it sound like I had done something wrong. Like I'd hurt him, by my absence or by ending things. "We had an agreement eight years ago. You were on board with it," I reminded him. I had never lied to him about the direction our non-relationship was going. Not once.

"I know that!" But the way he looked at me let me know that he didn't care what our agreement had been. He'd still ended up hating it in the end.

The same way I had.

We'd been so stupid.

I could see that now, but maybe now was too late. I left Eli to marry a woman I didn't care for all that much, and even though that marriage was over, the damage had been done.

"I'm sorry," I said softly.

Eli started walking again, and the dog looked at me in confusion until I followed. "It's fine," Eli said, and that word convinced me about as much as the last time he'd used it a few minutes ago.

"I wish you'd stop saying that when things really aren't fine."

"What do you want, Matt?" he asked without looking at me. "I can't do anything for you. I'm not sleeping with a married man."

I closed my eyes for a second and exhaled. "I'm not married anymore."

# Elias

"You're not?" I turned to face Matthew. Had he really just said what I thought he'd said?

Matthew spread his arms. "I'm divorced," he said as if it was no big deal.

Like hell.

"You can't just say something like that without following it up with an explanation!" I had so many questions. What had happened? When had it happened? And what did it all mean for me, if anything at all?

I could just *not* imagine Matthew getting a divorce. When he was younger, he'd always been very firm about knowing his duties as an alpha and his duties to his family and fulfilling them.

The one thing that had bothered me about him. How stubborn he was in his views of what an alpha needed to be. But unlike me, at least he'd known his place from the get go. It had taken me a painful lesson to learn mine.

"There isn't that much to say," Matthew claimed. His arms sank to his sides. "Danielle is a lovely woman and she was the perfect wife. She just wasn't perfect for me."

I raised an eyebrow at him. "She wasn't good enough for you?"

"That's not what I meant to say." He shook his head. "It's not that she wasn't good enough for me, we simply weren't good for each other, I think."

"The way we weren't?" I asked before I could stop myself.

He visibly cringed. "You know it's not the same." He took a step toward me, and I had to keep myself from taking a step back, because his proximity *did* things to me, even after all these years. He locked eyes with me and it was like all the days and weeks and months I'd lived without him vanished in a puff of smoke, making me feel like a kid again. Like a kid with a *crush*.

*God dammit.*

I drew in a breath.

"We had problems," Matthew said. "But compatibility was never one of them." His lips quirked up. "Neither was chemistry."

He came another fraction of an inch closer.

I stood still, heart pounding.

He pressed his lips to mine, and, without thinking, I leaned in. I couldn't help myself. This was *Matt*. And for one glorious moment, everything else ceased to matter.

Sadly, that moment didn't last longer than a second or two. Then reality came crashing back in.

What was I *doing?*

I had no idea, so I withdrew from Matt and

directed the question at him instead. "What are you doing?"

He gave me a small smile. "You never said what you'd do if I kissed you, so I figured there was only one way to find out."

"You're out of your mind!"

"And you liked it."

I bent down, grabbed some snow and flung it at him. He simply laughed while Fiona barked at the both of us.

"Okay, okay," Matt said eventually. "I won't kiss you again unless you ask me to."

I shot him a skeptical look. "Does that mean you'll be staying in town for a while?"

"That depends." Matt's expression grew serious again.

"On what?"

He licked his lips. "Tell me honestly, did you really get knocked up in college? Because I find that story hard to believe."

I swallowed. What was I going to say? I should have known he wasn't going to believe the rumors. I'd come here tonight knowing he might want to talk about the fact that I had a seven year old son, but even so, I wasn't sure what to do.

Tell him the truth?

Make up a lie?

I closed my eyes. No. He'd met Jake. He wanted to know, and even though I was scared of what was going to happen from here on out, I knew I couldn't keep the truth from him any longer.

"I wasn't knocked up in college," I said

eventually, looking at Matt again. "Those rumors are just that. Rumors. I never slept with anyone in college." How could I have? I'd been heartbroken.

"They say you don't know who your son's father is."

An unamused sound escaped my lips. "They say that because *they* don't know."

"But you do."

I took a deep breath and caught Matt's eye. "I didn't sleep with anyone for a long time after... "I gestured between us, words failing me.

From the expression on Matt's face, I couldn't tell what was going on inside him. He drew his arms around himself, maybe to be a shield from the cold, and he was quiet for a long time, as if he had to debate this news with himself before he could direct words at me.

"I never meant for you to find out this way," I said when the silence became too much.

That finally got him to talk. "What way did you want me to find out? Were you going to send me pictures from his college graduation?"

Ouch. I cringed, but I knew that his anger was totally justified. "I'm sorry."

"Why didn't you tell me?" he demanded.

"You were *married*," I reminded him. "I wasn't going to be the family-destroying omega. We had an agreement, remember? Each of us was going to live our own lives. You'd already moved on and I didn't want to drag you back. I didn't want to see you get disowned."

He grew quiet again, but this time, his silence

did not last as long. And when he spoke, his voice shook with suppressed emotion—mostly anger, I assumed. "You shouldn't have made that decision for me."

"No," I agreed, my own voice not completely steady either. "But I was young, and I was pregnant with the child of the man I loved, who had married someone else, and my life was falling to pieces around me and I wasn't making the smartest decisions. That's... not an excuse... but all I can say for myself."

Matt's expression softened the slightest bit. Although the lines of his face were still tight, he didn't seem *angry* now. Just... sad. I wasn't sure which was worse. "That's something else you never told me," he said.

I raised an eyebrow at him, because I didn't know what part he meant.

"You never told me that you loved me," he clarified.

"Would it have mattered?" I couldn't help but ask, because there'd never been any doubt about the temporary nature of our relationship.

He hesitated.

I forced a smile. "See, you can't even say. You weren't kidding when you said we had problems."

He shook his head. "I cared about you too. It just... took me far too long to realize." He exhaled. "I can't believe you got pregnant."

"Yeah... Neither could I. It's been eight years and I'm still wrapping my head around the fact." And I couldn't at all think about what might or might not have been if I'd told Matt earlier. I'd lose my mind if I did.

"I need some time to process this."

"Yeah... Sure..."

He walked away, and I didn't stop him. Even though I had so many questions burning on the tip of my tongue. Was he going to stick around? Did he want to help raise Jake?

Did he still have feelings for me?

Did I want him to?

I didn't know.

I really didn't know.

# Matthew

I was a father.

The thought stuck in my head and wouldn't leave. I had no idea how to handle this news. How did one react to becoming the father of a seven-year old over night? Was I supposed to be happy at the discovery? Angry that the secret had been kept from me for so long?

I didn't know. I just didn't.

I'd never been very in touch with my emotions, and this turn of events was entirely too much for me.

My breakfast tasted of nothing. I hardly realized that I was eating it as I tried to remember the boy's name. Jake, was it? It was a good name. Eli had chosen well, even without my input.

I sighed.

Eight years and not a single word. How could he?

"Are you listening?" my mother asked from across the table, one elegant eyebrow arched. I gave her a look. Had she been sitting there the whole time?

"I'm sorry," I said. "You were saying?"

She released a long breath, as if I was greatly inconveniencing her. A feeling she had been impressing on me my whole life, really. But that was just the way she was. *Everyone* inconvenienced her. Except maybe for my sister, who was really just a miniature version of her. Well, not so miniature anymore, I suppose.

"I was saying," she said with emphasis, "that your father requests your presence in his office when you've finished your breakfast. Although I really don't know why I have to deliver your father's messages now. As if I was a maid! Can you believe it?"

I shot the only maid within earshot an apologetic look. My mother often talked as if the staff couldn't hear her. "Thank you for telling me," I said, wondering what the old man wanted. I'd only seen him once in passing since I'd come home. My father had always been a busy man, and he'd never made a secret of the fact that my presence or absence in this house concerned him little.

I headed up to his office on the second floor as soon as I was done eating and knocked on the heavy door.

"Enter," came my father's gravelly voice from within. He sat in his large leather chair behind his large mahogany desk as I stepped into the room. I don't know if it was the size of the furniture that did it, but somehow, he appeared small to me. Smaller than he used to, anyway. His hair had receded and what was left of it had turned gray, and I had to admit that my old man really was becoming old.

"Mother said you had something to discuss with me," I said as I took a seat in the less-than-comfortable chair in front of his desk.

"I hear you got a divorce."

I swallowed. Sitting in this chair made me feel like I was a schoolboy again and receiving a scolding. "That is correct," I made myself say, because I *wasn't* a schoolboy anymore. I was a successful businessman, damn it.

My father furrowed his brows. "That is regrettable. And highly foolish of you. I must say, you disappoint me, son."

I grimaced. "Because I don't want to be with a woman I don't love?"

"Love, bah." He made a face. "You think I love your mother? I married her because it was the smart thing to do. Her family used to own some of the lands our hotels stand on today. I needed her for that and her uterus." He made a dismissive gesture. "What else are women good for?"

How to respond to that? I'd never thought that much about my parents' marriage. I hadn't necessarily assumed that they were in *love* with each other, but I would have liked to think that my father had a little more regard for my mother than that.

I really didn't know this man at all.

How was I his son?

"Your woman didn't even give you children," my father spoke on while I remained silent.

"I've been too busy to raise kids, anyway." Not that I wouldn't have made time if I'd known about Jake... but that was a different topic. And not anything I was going to discuss with my father.

He gave a dry laugh. "We are alphas. We sire children. We do not raise them."

What to say to that? My father certainly lived by those words. He hadn't raised me. My mother hadn't raised me. Their staff and expensive private schools had.

All so they could have heirs.

"You say that like it would be a bad thing to spend time with your children."

He shook his head. "My time needs to be put in the business so this family can prosper. No good comes out of an alpha thinking he has to waste his time doing a woman's job. Trust me, we don't have their instincts for handling children. It's all—"He stopped speaking to clutch his chest.

I stood from the chair. "Are you all right?"

He straightened again and waved me off. "It's nothing."

Was it, though? We alphas often ended up getting heart problems as we got older. Was that was this was? It would certainly explain why my sister was so concerned.

"In any case," my father continued. "You have to find yourself a new woman. Or let your mother find you one. And don't mess it up again."

"Certainly," I said, only because I didn't want to stress him, not when he'd been holding on to his chest a moment ago.

I excused myself from his office and left the house, intending to take a walk to clear my head.

Before I knew what I was doing, my feet had carried me into the town's center, and from there, it was only a short walk to Oceanport Elementary School.

I didn't linger by the school's fences, but I glanced across the schoolyard as I walked by, hoping to catch a glimpse of my son. I hadn't been able to get a good look. It had been dark, and I hadn't known that I was the boy's father back then.

There were no children on the schoolyard, though. They had to be in class, and I couldn't hang around until break time. People would start to wonder.

So I headed on, head full of questions. What was I going to do about Jake? If that day had taught me anything, it was that I couldn't use my own father as role model. Sadly, I couldn't think of anyone else in my life to imitate either.

I had to do *something*, though. I wasn't going to let Jake grow up like me—without knowing who his father was. No, I was going to be there for him. And I wasn't going to let my mother, my father, or even Eli stop me from that. Not any longer.

# Elias

"Dude, you actually told Matthew the truth?" My brother shot me an incredulous look while pouring coffee for us both after I'd put Jake to bed the day after I'd come clean about his parentage.

"Last night," I confirmed.

"And you waited until now to mention that fact?"

I shrugged. "I couldn't believe it myself. I mean... He asked me, and I... fessed up. Just like that."

Griff raised both eyebrows at me.

"Told you I couldn't believe it either."

Griff took a sip of his coffee and immediately grimaced, presumably because he'd burned his tongue. "How did he react?"

I laid my hands around my mug, as if to keep myself warm. "He got angry. At first, anyway. And then... I don't know. I think it was too much for him to process."

"It is a lot," Griff agreed. "I don't know what I'd do if someone told me I had a seven year old kid."

67

I sighed. "I have no idea what he plans to do now."

"What do you want him to do?"

Good question. "I'm not sure. Whatever's best for Jake. But I'm not sure what that is either. I don't really want to see him dragged into Matt's family." I shuddered, because they could do that. There were some old laws by which the child of an omega was the *possession* of whoever had sired it. *Especially* if it was an alpha. And I was sure that, if anyone, Matt's family were exactly the kind of people who'd use that to their advantage. They had the money to get all the lawyers they needed too.

My best case scenario was that they wouldn't want to have anything to do with the illegitimate child of an omega, but that was sad too. I'd rather Jake not know his relatives than know that they rejected his existence.

"Maybe you can run away together," Griff joked.

"Very funny."

He stuck his tongue out at me.

"I don't know who's more mature," I commented. "You or Jake."

My brother grinned at me. "Probably Jake."

"Yeah?" I cocked my head. "What makes you think so?" Not that I really needed a reason, but Griff looked like he had one. Which made me curious.

"He scolded me today."

I had to laugh, because I could picture it so well. My kid had strong opinions. "What did he scold you for?"

Griff mimicked Jake's voice. "Daddy says not to leave the fridge door open so long."

"That's my boy!" A smile took over my face and I almost forgot the serious topic we'd been discussing.

But Matt was right to be angry for missing out on this. For missing out on all the moments like this we'd had over the years. Missing out on *everything*. I stroked my hand back through my hair and sighed. I'd be mad if I was him.

But making this decision hadn't been easy for me either. I still remembered our very last night together so clearly. As if it had been yesterday. I'd never wanted to become too attached to Matt, but as our time together drew to a close, I *knew* that I'd messed up. All I could think about was that I wasn't going to see him again, not intimately, and that thought had *hurt*.

It had hurt so much it had been difficult to breathe when I dwelt on it.

And that night, after our last time together, I had no idea what to do about all these *feelings* I had as I watched him get dressed, my eyes lingering on the gorgeous patches of skin that were slowly being obscured from my sight.

Was I never going to see him naked again?

Feel the warmth of his skin against mine?

I bit my lower lip. Hard. I'd become way too used to this... *thing*... we'd been doing. Way too attached. It was a fling, right? Nothing more. It shouldn't hurt to see it end when I'd always known that it would.

Matt turned around to me, dark eyes catching

mine. "Are you okay?" he asked. Probably because I just sat there, unmoving.

I didn't know what to say. Was *he* okay? With all of this? "You're going to get married," I said. Not new information, of course, but there was no other coherent thought in my head.

He dropped his gaze, for only a second. "Yeah," he said then. "Weird, right?" He laughed, but the sound had something helpless to it. I'd never known Matt to feel helpless about anything, so I reached out to him, grabbed his arm and made him sit on the bed with me.

"Do you want to get married?" I asked.

He opened his mouth, then closed it again, looking at me as if he wasn't sure what to say. Another expression I didn't see too often on him. "I have to," he said eventually, with new resolve. "It's the right thing to do."

My heart sank, because Matt rarely backed down from a decision he'd made. His most alpha quality, probably. He was stubborn as hell.

The same way he'd been stubborn about pursuing me too. Leading me to this cabin in the woods again and again. He just wasn't stubborn about *keeping* me now that he had me, and I kind of wished he was.

I took a deep breath, because I wasn't going to cry. "I'm not going to see you again, am I?"

"Eli..."

"Is there any way we could...?"

Gently, he grabbed my chin and caught my eyes. There was sorrow in his gaze, but his expression was hard. "I'm sorry," he said, as he leaned in to kiss me, one last time and I tried to memorize the way his lips felt. Hard and rough and warm and soft all at the same time. "I'm going to miss you, Eli."

I swallowed through the lump in my throat. "I'm going to miss you too."

So, so much.

*You knew it was going to end this way.*

But that didn't make it any easier.

After that day, I'd only tried to talk to Matt again once. When I saw him in town during the winter holidays, but he'd been out with his new wife, and in the end, I'd never managed to work up the nerve to walk up to them.

Still deep in thought, I took a sip of my coffee. "He kissed me today."

"Who? Matt?" Griff shot me a confused look.

"Oh, did I say that out loud?" I shook my head.

"Yeah, you did!"

I pinched the bridge of my nose. "Well, it happened."

Griff gave me a conspiratorial grin. "How was it?"

I sighed. "Just the way I remembered it." Only more intense, because memories always faded after a while.

"Dude." My brother leaned forward a bit. "I thought you were over him."

I hid behind my coffee mug. "It's not that easy."

"Okay, okay. Did this kiss happen before or after you told him about Jake?"

"Before..." I furrowed my brows. "Of course it

was before. And I told him off for it. We really shouldn't be kissing." I set the mug down. "Nothing will come of it." After everything, I should know that.

"Yeah..." Griff leaned back again. "I guess you're right."

I took another sip of my coffee and then the phone rang. "I got it," I said, getting up to answer it. "Hello?"

"Eli?" Matt's voice greeted me on the other end. Immediately my heart rate sped up.

"Yeah, it's me."

"I thought a little about things." He paused, and I swallowed.

"So what are you thinking?"

"I have to see Jake."

I closed my eyes and inhaled. I couldn't keep Matt from his son, and I didn't want to, but how was I going to *explain* this to Jake? My mouth went dry. "I get that. I really do, but I don't know if Jake's ready for this."

"I understand. I'm not going to tell him anything if you don't think I should, not yet. But I need to see him."

Of course he did. "Yeah. Sure. That's fine." It was going to be fine. Just fine. *Deep breaths, Eli.*

"How about we take him sledding?" Matt suggested. "I got the impression he would like that."

"He would." Matt had really thought about this.

"Great. Saturday?"

"Great." And all I could do was repeat words.

"Alright. Then I'll fetch you Saturday around noon."

72

"You know where I live?" I asked.

"You're in the telephone book. How did you think I got this number?"

"Right. Okay. See you Saturday."

He hesitated. "...Eli?"

"Yeah?"

"I'm the one who needs to be nervous here, okay? You have nothing to worry about."

*Riiight.* "Okay," I said, although I didn't believe it.

Just as soon as we'd ended the call, I went up the stairs to Jake's bedroom. The door was left ajar so Fiona could go in and out as she pleased when she slept in his bed, as she often did. A bit of light fell into the room from the hallway, just enough to allow me to see my son's sleeping form from the doorway.

*Nothing to worry about. Right. Tell that to a parent.*

I took a deep breath. My messed up emotional state didn't matter here. Jake had a right to get to know his other father, and things were probably going to be fine. Probably. Did I want to hide him away from the world and everything that could hurt him? Hell yes. But that wasn't an option. I had to share my son with Matt and hope that everything would work out for the best. It didn't matter that being close to Matt was difficult for me. I had to be a grown-up about things.

Even if being a grown-up really sucked.

# Matthew

---◆◇◆---

Saturday turned out to be a beautiful day. The sun sat high in the blue sky and spilled her light brightly on the road ahead of us. For this special occasion, I had ditched my driver and taken the wheel myself. Mostly because I thought it was smarter not to let too many people know about me and Eli just yet. He wanted everything to stay low key for now, and if that was what he wanted, that was what he was going to get.

"Are we there yet?" Jake's voice came from the back of the car where he was sitting with his Daddy. His *other* Daddy. But it would take me a while to get used to that thought.

God, I couldn't believe that I had a son and that he was in the car with me. How was that even possible? I'd been childless just a few days ago.

"Not quite yet," I made myself respond. "But it's not far anymore." In the spirit of staying low-key, I'd looked for a sledding area a ways away from the town and anyone who would know us. It meant a bit of a drive. I didn't mind, but I hadn't considered how much patience a seven year old would have for this.

I knew nothing about children.

*No panicking, Matt.*

"I'm bored," Jake spoke up again. "There's a hill at your house. Why didn't we go there?"

*Because introducing you to my family would have been anything but low-key.*

I took a deep breath, wondering what to do and how to respond. In the end, it was Eli who saved me.

"Let's play a game," he said. "I spy with my little eye something beginning with C."

I exhaled as Jake began to guess and forgot all about his original question. I had to remember that game. Maybe learn some new ones too.

After a few more minutes in the car, we finally made it to the snow-covered hill. In the light of the sun, it looked so bright I almost wished I'd thought to bring sun glasses.

"We're here!" Jake, finally freed from the confines of the car, raced ahead. Eli went after him, and I was left getting the sled off the car. It was a wooden toboggan, large enough to fit all of us.

I caught up with Eli and Jake on top of the hill. There were a few other kids and their parents around, but no one paid us any mind. Perfect.

"This is nice," Eli said, hands in his pockets. It *was* a rather cold day.

Jake, meanwhile, had climbed on the sled as soon as I'd dragged it up. "C'mon, let's *go!*"

I had to laugh, because he reminded me of myself when I was a kid and I thought the world was mine for the taking. And so I climbed on the sled behind him.

"Daddy has to come too!" he insisted.

I looked at 'Daddy'. "Well?"

He exhaled. "Alright." Sitting behind me, he cautiously put his hands on my waist to hold on, and I realized why he'd been reluctant. Up this close, he wouldn't be able to escape the alpha scent coming off me, and I got a good whiff of him too. Almost immediately, hormones made my head spin.

Why had I thought sledding was a good idea?

"Everyone ready?" Jake called. "Here we go!"

And then we went, and I remembered why I'd picked sledding. For Jake. The kid was having so much fun. Laughing and cheering as the toboggan slid through the snow and down the hill. We'd barely made it to the bottom when he raced up again to have another go.

"Does he always have this much energy?" I asked Eli as we went after the kid. Our son. It was still weird to think that.

"Yeah. You should have seen him after he found my brother's secret chocolate stash and ate all of it when he was four." Eli chuckled, but his words made me feel a pang of bitterness.

"I didn't know he existed when he was four." How many more funny stories had I missed? How many important ones?

Eli dropped his gaze. "I'm sorry."

I got the feeling that he wanted to say more—*I* wanted to say more—but we'd already reached the top of the hill again and Jake was waving at us.

This time Eli went on the sled second, and I took seat behind him. Yeah, this felt a little more natural, and reminiscent of our youth, when we hadn't been sitting on a sled, but, well, doing other things pressed close together.

I closed my eyes and inhaled.

How could I still be into Eli?

But I was.

All of my irritation changed nothing about that fact. I still wanted him.

And as close as we were sitting, I could only *hope* that he wouldn't notice the evidence of that pressing him in the back.

I scrambled off the sled when we made it to the bottom of the hill again. Eli did too, but he didn't say anything to me, focusing on his son instead.

"Are you having fun?" he asked.

Jake threw his hands up. "This is awesome!"

I smiled. Maybe this whole parenting thing wasn't as hard as I thought it might be.

"I need a break," Eli claimed. "Why don't you go up again with Matt?"

What?

"No, you have to come too!" Jake insisted, as if speaking for the both of us.

"I'll come again in a little while."

Jake huffed. "Promise!"

"Promise." Eli patted his son's head. "Now

go."

"Okay." Jake looked at me and I started dragging the toboggan back up. He fell into step beside me, back to his energetic self.

It was sweet of Eli to give us some time alone, but I wasn't sure what to do with it, really.

*He's your son. Get to know him.*

Yeah, that sounded like a good idea.

"So you like sledding?" I asked, because *that* wasn't obvious.

"I love it!"

"What else do you like?" That was a better question. I mentally patted myself on the back.

He looked at me with his brown eyes—eyes the same color as mine—and made a thoughtful face. "I like cartoons. And swimming. But in the summer. Oh, and I'm going to be in the school play! That's going to be awesome!"

"The school play?"

"I have two lines!" he exclaimed proudly.

"Wow. That's a lot!"

"Yeah!" He beamed at me as we reached the top again and he climbed on the toboggan.

"Okay, hold on tight." I settled behind him and kicked us off again. Laughter burst out of him as we raced down the hill. I loved that sound. Made me feel like the best dad ever, even though I hadn't done much.

He was a great kid.

I found myself smiling as I climbed off the sled at the bottom of the hill—until something cold hit me in the back of the neck.

A snowball.

I turned around to find Eli, holding his hand to his mouth. "I was aiming for Jake, I swear!"

And before I even knew how to react, Jake jumped off the sled. "Snowball fight!" he declared, scooping snow from the ground. "C'mon," he said, looking at me. "He got you!"

Jake was right. This called for revenge.

I made a snowball with my hands and threw it at Eli. I didn't hit anything, but Jake did, cheering as the snow connected with his Daddy's face.

"Oh, you!" Eli threw more snowballs, but Jake quickly ducked behind me, so that *I* was the one getting hit again. Both of them laughed, as if this had all been planned.

"Sorry!" Eli said, still laughing. He was cute like that. I had always loved the way he laughed, like he was really trying not to but he just couldn't hold back and the sound just bubbled out of him.

I gathered some snow in my hand and approached him. "I'll give you sorry!" Quickly, I dropped the snow down his neck. He nearly shrieked.

"You asshole!"

Now it was my turn to laugh, watching Eli frantically try to shake the snow off. But I only laughed until Jake jumped up on my back, trying to do the same thing to me that I'd done to Eli. His sudden attack surprised me so much that I stumbled forward, taking Eli down into the snow with me.

Jake cheered on my back. "I got both of you!"

He climbed off, while I was still staring at the omega below me, his face only inches from mine and so, so kissable. I'd thought that about him from the moment I'd met him.

But I'd gotten better at controlling my hormones over the years.

So it didn't matter how much his lips begged to be kissed or how nice he smelled, I knew that I had to get up before the situation could get any more awkward than it already was.

Pulling myself together, I stood and held a hand out to Eli to help him up. He took it wordlessly. His hand was cold, but I was still loath to lose the contact when he let go again as soon as he got back on his feet.

Looking at me, he licked his lips, and I was expecting him to say something—when Jake pulled on his arm, breaking the tension.

"Look, Daddy!" He pointed at a couple of older kids on the hill. "They have tube sleds! Can I go with them?"

Eli gave the children a measuring look. "You have to ask them. Nicely!"

It was impressive how quickly he could go from confused omega to responsible father.

Jake nodded and sprinted off. Eli stuck his hands in his pockets and watched as his little bundle of energy approached the other children.

"He's not always good at social interactions," he muttered.

"He seems like a good kid, though."

The corner of Eli's lips tugged up and I saw so

much love in his eyes as he looked at Jake. "Yeah," he said. "Looks like he made it too."

Eli was right; Jake got on a sled with one of the older kids.

"You raised him well."

"I try," Eli said, eyes still on his son. "When I first had him I didn't know what to do either."

"Seems like you got a handle on things, though."

Eli shrugged. "What choice did I have? He needed me." After a moment, he pulled his smart phone out of his pocket. "There's... Something I think you should see." He tapped on his phone, and then held it out to me. On the display, I saw a picture of a baby. *My* baby, it had to be. What a weird yet wonderful feeling.

"Is that..."

"My brother took this picture just after Jake was born."

I stared at it. "I, uh..." Part of me wanted to ask him to send me that, but an even larger part of me couldn't get over how sad it was that I had to make a request like that because I hadn't been there for the birth of my son. I exhaled. "I can't believe I wasn't there."

"I'm sorry," Eli said. Again.

"Are you? Because it's been eight years, and if I hadn't run into you two, I still wouldn't know a thing. Would you prefer that? Because you could have told me at any time."

"Right." Eli's tone turned bitter. "Remember when I asked you if there was any way we could be together and you said no?"

I swallowed, because I *did* remember that. Not one of my favorite memories. I'd been stupid to start anything with Eli when I'd known it couldn't go anywhere. "That was different," I insisted. "I didn't know you were pregnant. If you'd told me—"

"Would you have given up everything?"

Eli's question caught me off guard. I wanted to say yes, just to be spiteful, but the truth was that I didn't know. I couldn't say for sure. I'd been young and stupid and so focused on my life's goals. But still... "I would have found some way to help you."

Eli laughed without a trace of joy in his tone. "Maybe I was okay with being your dirty secret, but I never wanted that for Jake."

"I don't know what to say." I only knew that I had so many regrets.

"I thought about telling you, you know. During the winter holidays, after I'd found out. But then I saw you with your wife, and..."

"Is that what made you back off?"

Eli averted his gaze. "Well, in part. I mean, it wasn't easy to see you like that. You looked happy. With her." He sighed. "You know, I'd been told all my life that one day, I was going to tear a family apart because that's what omegas do. We can't keep our legs closed and we breed like bunnies with no regards for the sanctity of marriage. I'd sworn to myself I wasn't ever going to be that stereotype, and yet..."

"Eli... you know our relationship wasn't like

82

that. I wasn't married when we were together. For that period of time, I was yours." *And long after, only you didn't know.*

Eli shook his head. "Doesn't matter. I knew you were promised to someone else. I had no illusions about that. But I still wanted you to be happy. And you looked happy," he repeated with emphasis. His breath caught on the last word and his eyes shone with unspilled tears. "I'm sorry I can't go back and make a different decision."

I took a step toward him and cupped his face. It didn't matter if part of me was still mad at him or not, I simply couldn't stand to see him in distress. "I'm sorry too," I said. "For so many things. I should never have left you in the first place."

"What are you saying?" Eli's voice remained remarkably steady, considering that a tear rolled down his cheek. I wiped it away with my thumb.

"I'm saying you're not the only one who makes stupid decisions every now and then."

"I never blamed you." He hesitated. "Well, maybe I blamed you a little. But I knew you didn't have a choice. Not really."

"No, that's what they want us to think. But we always have a choice." I looked into his eyes. Thankfully, no new tears were forming. Good. He had such pretty eyes. I could lose myself in them if I wasn't careful.

"You really think so?" Eli asked, looking up at me. He was just a little bit shorter than me. Ideal height, really. Perfect for me to lean in and...

"What are you doing?" I heard Jake's voice

from behind me.

Somehow I managed not to groan as I tore myself away from his Daddy.

"Nothing, buddy." I ruffled his hair, which had become a bit wet from the snow.

"Where's your hat?" Eli asked.

Jake patted his head as if only now realizing that he wasn't wearing it anymore. Then he looked behind himself and shrugged. "I don't know. I'll look for it!" And off he went again.

Only this time, Eli went with him and our moment was irreparably broken.

# Elias

———◆◯◆———

I spent the evening after Matt had taken us sledding sitting at the coffee table with a pen and a notepad in hand while Jake watched his favorite cartoons on the television. I was raking my brain for ideas about the charity event at the shelter, but it wasn't all that easy to think about cats and dogs when my mind was still stuck on how close I'd come to kissing Matt the day before.

Which would have been a stupid thing to do considering that he'd hurt me before. And considering that I still didn't know what he really wanted to do about our son. Who was my first priority in everything.

The commercials came on and Jake peered over my shoulder. "What are you doing?"

"Trying to plan a charity event," I informed him.

He shot me a questioning look.

"We're trying to get people to come to the shelter and give money to us so we can buy dog and cat food."

"Oh." He pulled his lower lip between his teeth as if thinking very hard. "Can you just ask them nicely?"

"Well, we are going to do that. That's good. But we also have to make them want to come to the shelter, you see? So they can see our animals and want to give."

"So the animals need to do something funny," Jake concluded.

"Well, not necessarily—"

"I'm sure everyone would come!"

His enthusiasm made me smile, even if it didn't convince me.

"When we went to the zoo, a lot of the animals weren't really doing anything," he said, crawling in my lap.

"What do you think they should be doing?" My curiosity was piqued. Jake had the darnedest ideas sometimes.

"I don't know." He looked up at me, poking his tongue out between his lips. "Something funny."

"You mentioned that." I ruffled his hair.

*That* seemed to give him an idea. His face lit up with it. "What if they all wear hats?"

"Hats?"

"Like the one you made for Fiona!"

Involuntarily, I grimaced. I'd only made the hat for Fiona because a younger Jake had insisted that if he had to wear a hat, so did the dog. Like every other omega, I'd had to learn knitting and sewing and crocheting. *Valuable skills*, I'd been told, and maybe they were, but I hated them. Learning all that had only taken time away from the things I'd really wanted to study.

"I don't know," I told Jake. "Fiona might become jealous if I knit things for other dogs."

He mulled this over for a second. "Fiona's a good dog," he decided. "She won't mind." He smiled. "Maybe you could make other clothes too! Like sweaters! It would be funny!"

I could tell my son was in love with this idea, even if I wasn't.

"C'mon, Daddy, write it down."

I gave in with a small sigh and wrote it down, hoping maybe someone at work had a better idea.

Jake grinned. "I'll tell all my classmates. They'll all come!"

"Great. Tell them to bring their parents."

But the commercial was over and Jake's attention was diverted.

Absentmindedly, I stroked his hair while he watched the continuation of his cartoon and I thought back to the day before. Jake had fallen asleep in the car on our way back, and Matt and I had talked a little bit. Not about anything serious, for the most part, but it had become clear that he wanted to see us again soon.

"Hey, Jake?" I tried when the cartoon was over.

He looked at me. "Is it bedtime yet?"

I glanced at the clock on the wall above the television. "In a few minutes, but I'd like to talk to you about something first."

He tilted his head, a curious expression on his face. "About the dogs?"

"No, not about the dog." I grabbed the remote control and shut the television off. "What do you think about Matt? Do you think he's nice?"

Jake gave me a half-shrug. "He's not very good at snowball fights."

"No, that's true. But he's okay, isn't he? He took us all the way to the big hill."

"Yeah." Jake looked back at the TV, even though it was off, and I could tell he wasn't super interested in this conversation. Why would he be? He didn't know that Matt was his father, and I wasn't at all sure how he was going to take those news when I finally told him.

"He suggested we go to the movies together next week. How would you like that?"

"I like the movies."

"Okay, then we'll go. And *now* it's bed time. Go brush your teeth."

"Do I have to?"

"You have to be good if you want to go to the movies."

"You're mean!" Jake complained, but climbed off my lap and headed toward the bathroom anyway.

\* \* \*

Jake enjoyed himself at the movies the next week. To my surprise, it seemed that Matt did too. No lies, I have to admit that I was a little worried about how much he would really like to see a children's movie, but he handled himself well and laughed at all the right moments. I couldn't tell whether he did that because he was genuinely amused or whether he was doing it for Jake, but I was grateful for it all the same.

It was kind of nice, being out like this. Almost as if we were a real family.

We weren't, of course. But maybe we could be. Someday.

It was a lofty dream, but one that I couldn't quite let go of now that Matt had reentered my life and he was getting along with Jake so well. He was making such an effort. That had to count for something, right?

I got the feeling that Jake was really starting to like him, too.

Still, there was doubt nagging at my heart.

Could I really let myself fall for Matt again?

The stakes were even higher now than they had been when we were younger. This time, if things went south again, that would hurt Jake too, if we weren't careful. And Jake had enough on his plate already.

Sitting in the back of the car with him on the way home from the movies, I kissed his hair. He'd fallen asleep again. Car rides always put him out when he was tired. It had been that way from the time he was a baby.

Slowly, I undid his seat belt as Matt parked the car in front of our house. Matt opened the door on his side and lifted the sleeping boy out.

"Be careful," I told him, even as the sight of

him holding my son—his son—tugged on my heartstrings.

"Of course."

I nodded and got out of the car myself, so I could open the front door of the house for Matt. That done, I led him inside and up the stairs. Then I showed him to Jake's room, turned the light on low and watched him lay our boy down on his bed and pull a blanket over him.

It was surprisingly quiet in the house, and I wondered whether Griff and Fiona were out on a walk or something, but wherever they were, I was selfishly glad for their absence. If only because it allowed me to see Matt watch our son sleep. And the expression of tenderness on his face told me all I needed to know about how serious all of this was to him.

Finally, he tore his gaze off Jake and studied the room instead, eyes trailing over the colorful drawings on the wall with interest.

"Why are there so many animals wearing clothes?" he wondered, and I could just keep myself from laughing. Afraid that the sound might wake our son, I took Matt's arm and led him out of the room. I closed the door to Jake's room before facing him again.

"Jake's got it into his head that I should do an animal fashion show at the shelter. Because I made that hat for Fiona, you know."

"Ah yes, that. It's a nice hat. But why should the shelter put on a fashion show?"

I shrugged. "We're low on funds. We need

donations."

"A charity event?" Matt cocked an eyebrow. "You should talk to my mother. She knows *all* about that sort of thing."

I gave a dry laugh. "Right. Me and your mother. Wouldn't that be fun?"

"It would be absolutely horrible. And probably boring. I don't think my mother's ever done anything as entertaining as an animal fashion show."

I shook my head. "It's just a crazy idea Jake had."

"Well, maybe you should do it."

I shot him a disbelieving look. "You really think so?"

"Why not?"

"I don't even really like knitting. I only learned it because I had to. It's an omega thing." I made a dismissive gesture with my hand—only to have Matt grab my hand in mid-air.

"Don't do that," he said.

"Do what?" I asked, trying hard to keep a clear head while I felt Matt's hand on mine and something about that single point of contact suddenly made me realize how close we were standing.

"Don't dismiss your talents because they're omega traits. There's nothing wrong with being an omega. And even if there was, you know that's not all you are. You've always been so much more than that."

I didn't know what to say to that. Matt

sounded so sincere. "I'm not the man you knew anymore. I couldn't do any of those things I'd planned. I couldn't even finish college."

"So what?" Matt took a step closer, and I had to take a step back because my heart was *already* going several miles a minute—but when I did, I found myself with my back to the wall.

Of course.

Matt gave me a small smile and I could tell by the way he looked at me that he didn't plan on granting me mercy from my hormones any time soon. "I don't care if you never finished college." He caressed my cheek with his thumb, and I shivered. "You raised a kid. And you did a damn fine job of it. That's no less impressive."

"You really think so?"

"Of course I do."

Matt leaned in, and almost, *almost*, kissed me—God I wanted him to kiss me—but at the last minute, he stopped. "I said I'd wait for you to ask," he murmured.

What? For a second, I didn't know what he was talking about. Until I remembered the kiss in the park, and the promise he'd made me after. He wanted me to ask him for a kiss. And I wanted to ask him, but I couldn't just do that. If I'd learned *anything* in my life it was that actions, especially actions like this, had consequences.

"There's something we need to talk about before we do this," I informed Matt.

He leaned back, a curious expression on his face. "So you're saying we *are* going to do this?

Because I've got to tell you, my mother keeps trying to introduce me to all these women, and all I can think about is you. This." He closed his eyes for just a moment and exhaled. And then when he opened his eyes again he looked right into mine. "I've never wanted anyone the way I want you."

His words, and the intensity with which he delivered them almost undid me, because I wanted him too, wanted to feel the weight of his body on top of mine, wanted to feel his naked skin touching mine—I'd *dreamed* of a moment like this for the past eight years—but there was something I needed to know before I could let this go any further.

I licked my lips, looking at him. "I want to kiss you. I really do, believe me, but... Are you... Is this..." I took a deep breath and started again. "Are you going to stick around? For Jake?"

*For me?*

The way his lips tugged up, just for a second, let me know he heard the part I didn't say. "I'm not going to leave Jake," he reassured me. And then, before I could respond to that, he leaned in again. And I pulled him closer.

# Elias

Somehow, we fumbled our way along the walls to my bedroom. It was a miracle neither of us tripped and fell or broke something, but we made it.

By the time Matt threw me down on the bed, all rational thought had fled my brain. I was a creature entirely controlled by raging hormones and driven by an insatiable desire for the alpha who'd stolen my heart so many years ago. The alpha whose mere scent still managed to drive me wild in ways I couldn't even describe.

For the most part, I was a calm and somewhat collected person. I really was.

Only Matt somehow managed to undo all of that within seconds. The moment I felt him on top of me, I was his. And there was something about this feeling of belonging, of being owned, that gave me a rush so strong it made me feel light-headed. Sometimes I wondered if it was some sort of hard-wired omega instinct that made me behave that way, but in the heat of the moment, I really didn't care. The feeling was way too good, too intense, for me to question it.

I'd had sex after Matt left, even with other alphas once or twice, but none of them had managed to get me into this state. Something had always felt *off*. Wrong, in a way.

But now as Matt claimed my lips and rocked our hips together, the only thing that bothered me was all the fabric between us.

I'd been wanting to have another night with Matt forever—no matter how foolish that was—and if we were going to do this, I wanted the full experience, not a dry-hump.

I ran my hand into Matt's hair and tugged just slightly. "You're wearing too many clothes."

"Yeah?" He gave me a slow, sexy smile. "Funny. So are you."

"Take them off me, then."

Matt's smile turned into a feral grin. "If that's what you want."

*If only you knew how* much *I want that.*

I raised my arms and lifted my legs helpfully as Matt tore my clothes off me like he couldn't get to the skin underneath fast enough. Like he wanted me as badly as I wanted him.

I hoped that was true, even if I still wasn't sure what that *meant* for us. I just wanted. Him. Us. This.

Once Matt had removed all the fabric from my body, he leaned down to kiss me again and I slung my arms around his neck while his hand roamed lower, trailing his fingers over my chest until they found one of my nipples. And Matt must have remembered how sensitive I was there because he started rolling the hardening nub between his fingers in a way that made my breath catch in my throat. He chuckled. The sound was a low rumble as he dipped his head to kiss my neck while his fingers continued to abuse my nipple in just the right way, his free hand finding the other one.

Oh God. It had been way too long since I'd let someone touch me like this. That fact alone would have made this experience intense, but on top of that, it wasn't just anyone touching me now—it was Matt! And I didn't know how to process that without letting a way too needy sound escape my lips.

"You like that?" Matt murmured. "You're going to *love* this then." And with that he enveloped my nipple with his mouth and teased it with his tongue.

I arched my back and moaned.

Matt laid a finger on my lips. "Don't wanna wake the kid, do you?"

"God no." I took a deep breath. "But you're not making this easy."

His lips curved up. "Guess I'll have to keep your mouth occupied."

"Guess you're—"

He shut me up by pressing his lips to mine. I closed my eyes and inhaled, drawing his scent into my nose. He smelled of alpha, and male sweat, and a little bit of the popcorn we'd had at the movies. The taste was on his tongue too, when it met mine, but only faintly. More than of popcorn, he tasted of *Matt*. He still tasted exactly the way he had when we'd first kissed in the woods all those years ago.

It was a taste I could never get enough of.

A taste I hadn't thought I'd have on my tongue again, and one that I'd missed so badly I never wanted him to stop kissing me again.

Dear lord, what was I getting into letting this alpha back into my heart?

Only he'd never really left my heart, and I lost my thread of thought when Matt ground our hips together.

I was already embarrassingly hard. And he was still wearing clothes!

I tugged his shirt out of his pants and ran my hands under it, feeling the warmth of his skin, and the way his muscles moved beneath it. He was still strong. I liked that. Turned on some primitive part of my brain like nothing else. I could run my fingers over the lines of his abs and pecs all day and not get bored. Hell, I could *lick* them.

Matt groaned when I lightly scraped my fingers over his nipples and finally took off his shirt. He was stunning to look at, just as he had been when we were younger. Alphas had an unfairly easy time keeping up a good physique, but I couldn't really be mad about that when it meant I got to feel all those muscles on top of me.

"Your pants too," I rasped.

He shot me a serious look. "Are you really sure about this?"

"Are you having second thoughts?" I asked,

eyes darting back and forth between his face and his groin, where I could see the outline of his cock stretching the fabric.

He shook his head. "I want you so badly it's all I can do not to jump on you."

"Is that why you still have your pants on?" I raised an eyebrow at him.

"It's the last thing standing between me and my desire to fuck you like we're animals."

"Oh yeah?" I licked my lips. "There's lube and condoms in the drawer to your right." And then, catching his eyes, I reached for his fly and undid it.

If *that* wasn't enough to tell him what I wanted...

Fortunately, though, it was.

He yanked his pants and his underwear off.

*Well, hello there.* I remembered that cock. Remembered exactly what it felt like inside me too. The memory was so intense now that I had it in front of my eyes that I felt oddly empty in my unfucked state. I *ached* to have that cock in me again. It was like the worst kind of itch, and definitely one I couldn't scratch myself.

When Matt found the lube and poured it in his hand, I spread my legs in invitation. I was a typical omega in that I didn't need a lot of preparation before sex, but if Matt was still the man I'd known, I knew he'd make sure I was ready anyway. And he did, sliding first one, then two fingers in and out of me while I did my best not to moan. I really didn't want to be heard by anyone else in the house.

"Harder," I said on a sigh, because his fingers couldn't satisfy me. Not when I knew what his cock was like. All his fingers did was tease, until the intensity of my need was almost unbearable.

And I'm sure the bastard enjoyed it too, watching me bite my lips to contain all the sounds I wanted to make.

And then finally, *finally*, he withdrew his fingers, rolled on a condom and entered me.

Shivers chased down my spine at the feeling of my hole stretching for him. The burn was minimal, but it was there, and I embraced it, spreading my legs even wider. Oh God, it was so good. To feel him again after all this time. I had to press a pillow to my face and bite on it to keep from moaning as Matt went in as deeply as he could.

After a moment, I felt the pillow being ripped away from me, and then Matt was there, kissing me. I welcomed him, letting his tongue into my mouth the same way I let his cock into my ass, feeling utterly claimed, owned and perfectly happy.

It was a confusing feeling when I wasn't being high on it. And Matt was the only one who could push me into this state. He was my drug.

No wonder I'd fallen to pieces when he left.

Unconsciously, I dug my fingers into his back. He made a low noise in the back of his throat, and then he started moving, putting a stop to all my thoughts.

He went as fast and hard as he could in our position, keeping his lips pressed to my mouth. I bucked my hips, wanting more, always more. My body shook a little every time he hit my prostate, sparks of need tearing through my self-control. I moaned into Matt's mouth, utterly unable to keep quiet.

After another minute, he gave me the pillow back, leaned up a bit to grab my hips and started really pounding into me.

I was glad for the pillow. Without it, I would have woken not only my kid but everyone in the neighborhood.

Matt hadn't lied when he'd said he wanted to go to town on me. Every thrust came hard and deep. He was wrecking me. And I loved it.

If it hadn't been for the pillow, I would have begged him for more. I nearly sobbed when I felt his large hand wrap around my cock. It was almost too much. I didn't want to come yet, I wanted to ride this feeling forever, but there was no way that I could hold back. Once Matt started stroking me in time with his thrusts, I was done for. I struggled to hold back the flood, but the waves came crashing over me anyway. I bit the pillow hard as my orgasm tore through me like a force of nature until I was absolutely spent.

Above me, Matt groaned in a way that let me know he was done too. I laid the pillow aside and closed my eyes as he embraced me a moment later. After the intense climax I'd just had, his arms around me felt like the only thing holding me together. And I was strangely okay with that—even as part of me wondered whether I was setting myself up for more heartbreak.

Oceanport Omegas

# Elias

The next morning, my brother was already in the kitchen making coffee when I got up. That was a rare occasion. Usually, he liked to sleep late. But that was not the only thing different about him that morning. He seemed... awfully jumpy when I entered the kitchen.

"Something wrong?" I asked, when he almost dropped the mug he was getting out of the cupboard upon hearing me step inside.

"No!" He whirled around to me. "Nothing. How was your night?"

I raised an eyebrow at him. "How was *your* night?" Come to think of it, I hadn't heard him come home. "You were out pretty late, weren't you?" I gave him a grin. I liked the thought that he might have been out with someone. These days, that rarely happened. My brother only two years younger than me, but as far as I knew, he was still a virgin.

And right now, he was blushing like one too.

102

"It wasn't *that* late."

I stepped up to him and patted him on the back. "Nothing to be ashamed of," I told him. "You really should get out more." Honestly, I felt a little guilty sometimes that my brother didn't have more of a social life. There was a myth floating around that some people believed and which said that omegas should be virgins until their matings because apparently we *imprint* on the first guy we sleep with and never get over him.

That was crap, of course, but since I'd never really moved on from Matt, I feared Griff might be wondering if there was something to it. And that sort of pressure could ruin any budding romance.

"I'm not ashamed," Griff said, pouring some coffee into his mug. "Nothing happened."

"Fine." I grabbed a mug for myself. "But you know it'd be cool even if something had happened."

"I know," he insisted and then he pressed his lips together.

"Okay, I won't talk about it anymore." I turned away from him to sit at the table. "But even if your night was uneventful, mine wasn't."

"What do you mean?" His eyes grew wide. "Wait, did you and Matt...?"

I laughed a little, because I wasn't sure how else to react. "Yeah, it kind of just happened."

Griff sat at the table with me. "So... what does this mean now? Are you getting back together?"

"Honestly? I don't know. It sort of... sounded like that. I asked him if he was going to stick around. I meant for Jake, but... you know. I didn't *just* mean for Jake. I think he got that." Or did he? I hadn't been super clear the night before. It was difficult to be super clear when your brain was doused in hormones.

"You should really talk about that some more."

I sighed. "You're probably right."

"Have you thought about when you're going to tell Jake?"

"About the relationship or...?"

"You know what I mean."

I grimaced. Of course I knew. We had to tell Jake the truth about his parentage, and we couldn't wait much longer. The longer we waited, the weirder it would probably get. "It's just such a difficult topic. I'm not sure how to approach it."

"Yeah, I get that." Griff gave me a sympathetic look. "But I think you should tell him soon."

"Yeah, well." I ran a hand through my hair and stood from the table. "For now, I have to wake him up and get him to school."

\* \* \*

I went into work that day with my head held high. Something about talking to Matt the night before had bolstered my spirits, and I could still feel it as Harold sneered at me when I walked into the shelter.

"Something wrong?" I asked him. "I'm not late this morning."

"You should be worried you even have to

mention that," he waved me off. "Did you come up with anything for the event? The boss wants to talk to both of us again."

"I... have an idea." Harold probably wasn't going to like it, but that wasn't my problem, was it? I was just doing my job. A job that I was actually really good at.

My brother's words came to me again. That I needed to get out of here, do what I'd really planned to do with my life.

Maybe it wasn't too late after all.

Maybe I could still go back to school and be more than *just an omega*.

Matt thought I was more.

"What are you thinking about?" Harold asked. "Staring into space like that. Get to work."

I was tempted to stick my tongue out to him, but I didn't. Not even Harold could ruin the nice day I was having. I wasn't going to let him.

In reality, I even kind of enjoyed the expression on his face when the boss called us into his office later and I told him what I'd thought about for the charity event.

"An animal fashion show?" Harold spat. "No way I'm going to be doing that. That's for sissies and omegas."

"Well," I said. "I'm an omega." *And not ashamed of that fact. Not today.*

"Fine. Then you can do it!"

I looked to my boss, who turned to Harold. "Did you have any good alternative ideas? Because I believe if we did this well it could draw people in.

The Omega's Secret Baby

I'm thinking of maybe having an auction afterward." He leaned back in his chair and scratched his chin. "Yes, yes, that could work, I believe."

Harold's eyes widened. "You can't be serious."

But he didn't offer a better idea.

"Look," I said, turning to him. "I don't need your help making the outfits or anything." I doubted that he could knit anyway.

"Well, you won't get it!"

"Fine!"

"Are you sure you can do this by yourself?" my boss asked, one eyebrow raised. "Because to be honest, I couldn't help you with the knitting either. But I guess it pays to have an omega on staff for things like this."

It was difficult not to grimace, hearing those words. This was all I was to my colleagues, wasn't I? *The omega on staff.*

Again, I had to think of filling out a college application. People might finally take me seriously when I had a *Dr.* in front of my name. And if Matt helped raise Jake...

This might actually be feasible.

"I'm sure I can do this," I told my boss. Because, really, it was time to man up. About this charity event, and everything else.

"Good, good."

I left my boss's office in high spirits.

And I should have known that the day couldn't possible continue to go that well. I was hardly out of my boss's office for ten minutes before my cell phone began to ring. And that usually only meant one thing.

Jake's school.

Of course.

I sighed, and answered the phone, although I really didn't want to. What had my little bundle of energy done this time?

"Mr. Stevens?"

"Speaking."

"We'd like for you to come down to the school, please. It's about your son Jake. Honestly, it's much the same thing I called you for last time."

The same thing? *Oh, c'mon.* I'd really hoped Jake had learned his lesson. "Did he get into another fight?"

"Well, if it's any consolation to you," the secretary said, "this time they were both throwing punches."

No, that wasn't really much of a consolation. "I'll be down there as fast as I can."

* * *

I went down to the school, I listened to what the principal had to tell me, I apologized profusely, ignored the way Mrs. Foster glared at me, and then I took my son, put him in my car, and drove all the way home in complete silence.

I couldn't talk to him. Not yet. I knew the moment I opened my mouth, I would explode. How could he do this again? Like I didn't have enough on my plate.

Like *he* didn't have enough on his plate.

I parked the car in front of our house and together, we walked inside.

"Oh, it's you guys!" my brother greeted us from the living room. He poked his head in the hallway. "Anything wrong?"

"Why don't you ask your nephew what happened," I said, taking my coat off. Thankfully, I didn't have to go back to work that day, so that was one less thing to worry about.

Jake looked at Griff, lips pressed in a thin line and shoulders hunched, as if he was being unfairly accused or something. "I got into a fight," he said eventually. "With a mean boy."

Griff sighed. "Again?"

"He started it." Jake pouted.

"Oh yes," I chimed in. "The other boy was the first to punch. After you took his sandwich and tossed it in the trash."

"He said—"

"I don't care what he said," I cut Jake off. "I don't care at all, okay? We had an agreement, and you broke it."

Jake stared at the floor and said nothing, and I got the feeling that I wasn't getting through to him.

"You got yourself suspended!" I went on. I was sure he was aware of this, but I had to vent, anyway. "Do you want them to throw you out of the school? You like the school, don't you?"

"I don't like the school!" Jake burst out. "I hate the school! And I hate you!" With that, he stormed up the stairs, still in his street shoes.

"Jake!" I called after him, but he was already throwing the door to his room shut.

I took a deep breath, which didn't calm me at all. Some days it was just a joy to be a parent.

# Matthew

The day after I went to the movies with Eli and Jake, I had tea with Frederica again. She said she had something to tell me. Something that she could only tell me if I made time for her, though. Since I liked Frederica, I didn't exactly mind being blackmailed like this, but I did wonder what kind of news she had for me.

Frederica however, liked to keep the suspense alive.

And so we sat at a table in the one of the smaller living rooms in my parents' mansion while she calmly sipped her tea and talked about the weather.

"There's going to be more snow, you know."

"Really?" I gave her a forced smile. "Frederica, you know I love our conversations, but could you please tell me what you really wanted to talk about?"

The corner of her lips tugged up. "Oh, sure I could. I'll tell you what I know as soon you tell me what you know."

"What do you mean?"

She rolled her eyes. "I'm talking about your omega and his boy, of course." She made a disapproving face. "You never told me if you found out whether he's yours or not."

Oh, that. I'd thought a lot of Eli and Jake lately, but I hadn't thought about Frederica in any of this. I'd simply had too much on my mind lately. "I did find out," I told her. "But I can't share this with you unless you promise me again that you won't tell a soul about this." I couldn't stress that enough. If rumors spread about this... That would hurt both Eli and Jake.

Frederica sighed. "I know. I know. You won't let me have any fun."

I gave her a hard look.

She shook her head at me. "You know I'm just joking. I won't tell anyone." She set her cup down. "I won't deny that I love rumors, but I care about you too."

That was touching. I'd often thought that Frederica was like a mother to me, but we didn't normally speak of it. But I knew that I could trust her. Even with this.

I took a deep breath and leaned forward. "The boy is my son." And it still felt surreal to say that.

Frederica raised a hand to her mouth. "Is he really?"

I nodded.

"Oh my God. I can't believe you're a father." She looked so ecstatic I half expected her to jump from her chair and hug me, but she didn't. Instead she took a large gulp of her tea. "You're really a dad. I can still picture you when you were two, and now you're all grown up."

"I was all grown up before I told you this."

"This is different." She waved me off. "Now you're a parent."

I exhaled. "I know. But just because I know that I have a son now doesn't..." I struggled to find the words.

"Doesn't what?"

"It doesn't mean that I know how to be a parent."

Frederica nodded. "No, I guess not. This must be a lot to take in." She leaned back in her chair. "But any way, I'm sure you'll do a much better job of it than your sister. Did you hear she's coming over today with that little brat of hers? What's your son like? Please tell me he's not as bad."

I actually had to laugh a little. Leave it up to Frederica and her odd way of leading a conversation to cheer me up. "He's nothing like my nephew, I assure you. He *is* a little alpha, though."

"Is he? Isn't he only seven?" Frederica shot me a curious look.

"Yes, I know it's early to tell, but he's definitely an alpha."

"Taking after his dad." Frederica gave me another smile. "You were trouble too."

"I was not."

"Oh yes." She took a sip of her tea. "Remember that time you insisted all the children

112

coming to your birthday party had to be dressed as clowns? I was finding thrown away red noses all over the house for weeks."

Oh God. I had forgotten all about my childhood obsession with circuses.

"You were a stubborn child," Frederica said. "And you've grown into a stubborn man."

Had I? In some regards, perhaps. But being stubborn wasn't always a bad quality.

"You should bring the boy around some time," Frederica went on. "I'd like to meet him."

I grimaced. "Bring him here and introduce him to my parents?"

"Oh no, maybe not such a great idea. You're right." Frederica shot me a sympathetic look. "But you're not going to keep him a secret forever, or will you? You know I love a good secret."

"No, I won't." That wouldn't be fair to Jake. It wasn't that I was *ashamed* of him or anything. I just didn't want to expose the child to my parents quite yet. "I'm not sure what I'm going to do. This has all been... difficult."

Frederica nodded. "But you're going to raise him?"

"I do want that. But like I said, I don't know how to be a parent yet."

"I'm sure you'll be fine. Nobody knows at first. You grow into it."

I could only hope she was right.

But there wasn't only the issue of whether or not I knew how to be a parent. There was also the issue of whether or not Jake was going to accept me as such. After all, we still hadn't told him about any of this.

And I couldn't stay in town forever either. At some point, I would have to go back to work. For now, I was managing things via the Internet, but that was only a temporary solution. The reality was that I had built my life in a different state.

I took a deep breath, and a sip of my tea.

No use worrying about all of that now.

"What were you going to tell me?" I asked Frederica.

She shot me a questioning look, as if she'd already forgotten why she'd summoned me in the first place.

"Your news," I reminded her.

"Oh, yes!" She reached out to refill her tea before going on. Then she licked her lips. Never a good sign. Whatever she had to tell me, it wasn't good news.

Just great.

Because I really needed more problems now.

"Well," Frederica started. "You know how people like to talk." She waved her hand dismissively as if she wasn't one of those people, even though we both knew she was.

"I know. Go on."

She gave me a tight smile. "There's a rumor going around about you and a certain omega."

"Me and a certain omega?" My eyebrows shot up. Eli and I had tried so hard to be discreet.

Her expression turned to one of sympathy. "You were seen going into his house last night. And not coming out for a while."

"That was last night! And you already know about it?" This was *exactly* why I'd been glad to leave this place for my boarding school at the end of summer each year.

She shrugged. "It's a small town. People talk. They don't have much else to do. You know how they are."

I pinched the bridge of my nose. "How bad is it?"

"Well, everybody thinks you slept with him. Little Rosie from the bakery even thinks you paid him for it, but that girl has always been a bit dumb."

I groaned. "Do I really look like I need to pay people for that kind of thing?"

"Oh no, you don't. You're an attractive young alpha. Like I said, Rosie's just dumb." Frederica gave me a smile before her expression became more serious again. "Everybody else believes that Elias seduced you. You know it's natural to blame that kind of behavior on the omega. Especially on one who's been unmated for so long and who doesn't know the father of his child."

I sighed. *Those stupid...*

Eli deserved so much better than this.

"It was always me," I told Frederica. I'd been the one to go after him when we were younger, and I was the one who'd kissed him this time. If people wanted to blame anyone, they should be blaming me. I just couldn't control myself around Eli. Hell, I didn't *want* to control myself around Eli. Being with him just felt so much better than anything I'd ever experienced. When we were together, everything felt *right* in a way that I couldn't even explain.

"I have no doubt about that," Frederica said with a twinkle in her eye. "If you saw him and you decided that you wanted him... Poor boy never stood a chance."

"Yeah... The first time I took him out, we went out into the woods to walk this dog I'd found... He told me about how much he loved animals and all he wanted to do in the future. He wanted to become a vet, you know? He'd worked really hard for his scholarship." I'd been impressed, and I'd had no idea that I was leading him down this path when I eventually pushed him up against a tree just to kiss him. I had to make this right. Somehow. "Those rumors... Are they also about Jake?"

Thankfully, Frederica shook her head. "No. They haven't made that connection. Not yet, anyway."

I grimaced again, because she was right. It was only a matter of time before people would come up with the wildest theories. And it would be best if Eli and I figured things out between us before we had the whole town trying to take part in that conversation.

I drank the last of my tea, wondering how to approach this topic with Eli when a maid knocked on the door. I turned to her, one eyebrow raised.

She cleared her throat. "Your mother would like you to join her in the sitting room. Your sister has arrived."

116

I did my best to smile at the maid instead of groaning. "I'll be there in a minute."

I had no doubt what those two wanted to talk to me about.

And I only had to spend five minutes in the sitting room, watching my mother and sister exchange fake smiles while my nephew stared at his smart phone to be proved right.

"Darling," my mother addressed me. "Your sister informed me that she knows a very lovely lady in search of a husband."

"Oh, yes?" I asked. "And how would my wedding to this lovely lady contribute to the family wealth?"

"Oh, don't be like that." My sister glared at me while my mother's eye brows arched up as if she just couldn't believe the words coming out of my mouth. But I was so tired of this little game of pretend my family liked to play. We all knew why my mother wanted me to marry again, so why beat around the bush?

"Be like what?" I asked my sister.

"Difficult," she said, shaking her head. "Marianne wouldn't give you any trouble if you married her, and you'd be doing something good for all of us."

*Wouldn't give you any trouble.* Was that really the best I could aim for in a relationship? I felt almost bad for my sister that she didn't see the problem with that.

*That's only because she hasn't met someone she really loves. Not like you did.*

117

"Listen to your sister," my mother said. "She's trying to help you."

I had to keep myself from snorting, because I knew what my sister was *really* trying to do. Grow the wealth and influence of our family because she thought her smart phone obsessed brat was going to inherit it all one day. She was exactly like our mother, doing what she thought was best for her offspring, however misguided her ideals were.

"I'm really not in the mood for this right now," I said, stroking a hand through my hair. "I'm still trying to get over my divorce."

"Oh?" My sister put her hands on her hips. "The divorce you asked for, you mean? Yeah, Mother has told me everything, and you clearly haven't been making the best decisions. We're just trying to help you get back on track."

"Of course you are." I couldn't keep the sarcasm out of my voice, and I have to admit that I didn't try very hard either. "I assure you I'm fine. And I will deal with things in time."

"I'd just rather you deal with this before Father has to step down."

"Karen!" Mother reprimanded her. "You weren't to speak of this."

I looked at both of them. Good to know my family was definitely keeping secrets from me. "Are you going to tell me what this is about?"

My mother's lips formed a thin line. "This is not a conversation I want to be having now." And before I could stop her, she simply left the room.

Sighing, I turned to my sister.

"Look what you did!" she said. "You really shouldn't be stressing Mother like this on top of everything else she has to deal with already."

"Cut the crap," I said. "I know why you really want me to marry, and I'm telling you, it's not going to happen." Not now or anytime soon. I was done marrying people my family thought were good for me.

"Where's your sense of duty?" she asked me. "I thought you alphas were all about protecting your family."

"That doesn't mean I can't care about my own life."

"Fine then, go ahead, be selfish."

I shook my head at her and left the room. She wasn't completely wrong about what she'd said. I did feel the need to protect my family. But our conversation had made me realize something. When I thought of my family now, I didn't think of her or our parents. I thought of the most caring, most handsome omega and an energetic seven year old boy who had my eyes.

# Matthew

After that conversation with my family, I went out into the snow covered gardens to cool off. My family upsetting me was nothing new. Every time I came for a visit, be it on a school break or on a holiday from work, we found something to fight about. I'd found ways to deal with it. When I was younger, for a little while, my way to deal with stress had been Eli.

And to this day, I hadn't found a better way.

For some reason, I couldn't stay stressed around him. It was as if he could reach into my soul and soothe the tension away with just a look, a touch of the hand. I had no idea how he did it, but it was incredible.

So of course I thought of him now. When I was being honest, he'd never been far from my mind since I first ran into him all those years ago. Not even when I'd been married to Danielle.

It was one of the reasons I'd known I had to break up with her.

I just wished I had come to that realization a little bit sooner. Like, a few years sooner.

I wanted to talk to him, make plans for our future. Big plans. I never wanted to leave him again. I knew now what a mistake that had been.

I just wasn't sure how to fix my mistake without causing the man I loved any more pain. Maybe it was too late for that. The whole town was talking already. It wasn't fair that Eli had to be suffering for something we'd both done. Something that wasn't even a *bad* thing.

We *loved* each other, I was sure of that. It was just the circumstances we lived in and everyone's prejudice complicating it all.

Tilting my head back, I looked up into the sky. It seemed like we were going to get more snow. I took a deep breath and fished my phone out of my pocket. I already had Eli's new number memorized, and I dialed it without thinking.

He answered the phone on the third ring. "Hello?" It was silly, and probably not something an alpha should be admitting, but just the sound of his voice made me feel a little better.

"Hey, it's me."

"Oh, hey." Eli's voice softened.

"I was wondering whether you and Jake might want to do something tonight." After the fight I'd just had with my family, all I wanted to do was surround myself with the people who *really* mattered.

"Well, I'd love to, but Jake's grounded." The way Eli sighed let me know how annoyed he was with his son. Our son.

"Did he get himself in trouble?"

"You could say that." Eli paused, as if considering how much he wanted to tell me.

"Will you tell me what happened?"

"I guess you *should* know," he said, finally. "It's just... it's stupid. He keeps getting into fights with one of the boys in his school."

"Physical fights?"

"Yeah. Fists flying and all. The first time he did this was actually the day we ran into you at the park. He'd promised me not to do it again, but his school called me today at work because apparently he just couldn't keep that promise."

I grimaced. "He has too much energy." And I remembered exactly what that felt like, although it hadn't been an issue for me until my teenage years.

"I only wish he'd find other ways to release it. I've tried talking to him, but he won't listen. So yeah, he's grounded. He also got himself suspended from school for the next two days. And they won't let him take part in the play anymore either."

"That's too bad. I got the feeling he was really looking forward to that."

"He was." Eli sighed again. "But I do agree with that decision. He's got to learn that his actions have consequences." And in a smaller voice he added, "Imagine if we had learned that before getting together."

His words gave me pause. "Are you saying you'd rather we'd never met?"

"No!" he said quickly. "I mean, I don't know."

He seemed to struggle with how to go on while I waited with bated breath. "You have to admit we didn't exactly... we weren't smart about what we were doing."

"Yeah, you're right about that part." I ran a hand through my hair. He *was* right. Not much I'd done when I was with him had been smart. I liked to think of myself as a somewhat intelligent person, but when I was around Eli, especially when I'd been younger, rational thought tended to fly out the window.

"I enjoyed our time together," Eli said. "I really did, so... I don't know. I'll be honest with you. There have been moments when I thought that it would all be better if I'd never met you. Like, when I first found out that I was pregnant. Or when Jake was a baby and he wouldn't go to sleep and I was tired and I couldn't find a job."

"I'm sorry." It was all I could think to say.

"Don't be. I should have just... let you know about all this a lot earlier. And I... don't regret any of it. I don't regret us. I wouldn't want to lose those memories. And I couldn't imagine losing Jake. Even when I'm mad at him like I am right now." He gave a tiny laugh that made me smile.

"I'm glad." I closed my eyes for a moment, thinking of the days I used to sneak out of this house to be with Eli. "I wouldn't want to lose those memories either. Not a single one."

"I still remember every day," Eli said softly.

"Me too." I looked to the sky again, and for a minute or two, neither of us said a word, lost in memories. I wasn't lying to Eli. I did remember it all. I still do.

"Do you still want to come over?" Eli asked after a moment.

Did I? People were *already* talking about us. If I went to Eli's place now, the second night in a row...

I huffed, annoyed with myself. If Eli wanted to see me, I had to go to him, and maybe I could help. "I would love to come over."

\* \* \*

When I entered Eli's place, I was greeted by an enthusiastic dog at the door. "Hey, Fiona." I dropped to one knee to ruffle her soft fur. "I've missed you too!" I'd thought about getting a dog once or twice, but Danielle wasn't a big fan, and I spent too much time at work anyway.

"Maybe we should go into the living room," Eli suggested. "Once Fiona lets go of you, I mean."

I gave him a smile. "Oh, I already have plans for when Fiona lets go of me."

He shot me a quizzical look. "Yeah?"

"Yeah." I grinned at him and freed myself from the dog, getting up. Taking a step toward Eli, I pulled him into a kiss. He made a small sound of surprise, but leaned into me after another second like it was the natural thing to do. When I let him go again, he smiled at me.

"That was your plan?" he asked.

"Yeah. Giving you a proper greeting."

He licked his lips. "I could get used to that."

"You should." And my eyes were stuck to his lips. I wanted to take him upstairs and extend this greeting a bit, but then I remembered who else was probably upstairs and why I'd come here. "Is Jake still in his room?" I asked.

"Yeah." Eli glanced at the stairs. "I don't think he's going to come out of there anytime soon. He might be only seven, but he's stubborn." Eli shook his head. "It's impossible to deal with him when he gets like this until he snaps out of it."

"Do you think I could talk to him?"

"You?" Eli's eyebrows shot up.

"Don't look so surprised. I'm..." I lowered my voice. "I'm his parent too, right? Maybe I can help with this."

"You really think so?"

I shrugged. "I'm an alpha. I think I know how he feels."

"Alright. If you really think you can help."

"I do." At least, I hoped I could help. When I was being honest, I still had no idea whether I could be a parent. But I was about to find out. Taking a deep breath, I took a step toward the stairs when Eli stopped me.

"Just..."

I turned to him. "Just what?"

"Nothing. Just..." He folded his arms in front of his chest. "Just don't scream at him or anything."

"That's not what I was going to do." He was only a seven year old boy after all. I didn't need to scream at children to assert dominance, even if some alpha stereotypes would have you believe so.

"I'm sorry." Eli unfolded his arms and ran a hand through his hair. "I get overprotective. He's my baby."

I gave him a smile. "It's nice to know omegas can get overprotective too."

"Yeah, well." He creased his brow in what I could only assume was supposed to be a defiant expression. "Try to hurt my baby and see what happens!"

I had to laugh. He looked so adorable when he tried to be threatening. "Okay, okay. I'll be careful."

"Thank you."

"Don't worry." I gave him a quick kiss before I turned to the stairs again. *Here goes nothing.*

When I reached Jake's room, I tried knocking on the door. It took a moment, but then I heard his voice from inside.

"I don't want to talk to you."

Eli really hadn't been kidding about the little one being stubborn. But I'd been a stubborn kid myself.

"Really?" I asked. "It's me, Matt."

Jake's voice turned curious. "What are you doing here?"

"I wanted to have some fun with you and your daddy."

"Daddy won't let me play."

"Yeah, I heard about that. Hey, would you mind if I come in so we could talk about that? Then maybe I can convince your daddy to let you play. How's that sound?" I caught myself thinking that this really wasn't too different from being in a business negotiation. If my business partners were children who could be tempted with an offer of play time.

"Okay," Jake said, opening the door.

So far so good.

I stepped into his room and made a show of looking around while he closed the door behind me. "Really nice room you have here. Did you do all these drawings yourself?"

"I did. Well, except for that one." He pointed to a drawing of a dinosaur that hung by the door. "Daddy did that one and gave it to me. Because I gave him so many drawings."

"That's nice." I studied the image. If Jake hadn't told me, I'd never have guessed that an adult had drawn it. It was a good thing Eli had other qualities.

I sat on Jake's bed and he settled next to me.

"What were you doing before I came?" I asked.

He showed me a book that lay beside his pillow. It seemed to be a story about dinosaurs.

"You really like dinosaurs, huh?"

He shrugged. "They're cool. But I want to play outside now."

"Yeah, I get that. It's nice outside." I could see a clear sky through the window.

Jake drew his knees toward himself and rested his head on them.

"Would you like to tell me what happened?" I tried.

"I got into a fight at school."

"How did that happen?"

"Miles was being mean. So I took his sandwich and threw it away. Then he punched me. So I punched him. But I didn't start it!"

"No, I'm sure you didn't." I rubbed my chin in an effort to look like I was giving this a lot of thought. "Your daddy told me you made him a promise that you weren't going to punch other kids anymore."

Jake looked away, so maybe that hadn't been the right thing to say.

"He's very sad that you broke your promise," I tried, because I got the feeling that Jake cared about Eli. Especially if our first encounter was anything to go by. My kid was an alpha, and he wanted to protect his dad. He wouldn't like the idea of him being sad because of something he'd done.

And I was right. Jake turned to me again. "Is he really?" he asked softly.

"Of course he is. He doesn't want you to get into trouble. He's worried about you."

"He doesn't have to worry about me!"

I almost had to laugh because of how sincere Jake sounded. Quite the little grown-up. "He will always worry about you, even if you become a big boy."

"I'm already a big boy!" Jake pierced me with his eyes.

I reached out and ruffled his hair. "Of course you are. But that doesn't change anything. You upset your daddy."

"I didn't want to do that." He looked aside, letting his hands drop.

"I'm sure it'll be fine. You only have to stop punching other children."

"I didn't even start it this time! What should I have done?"

"Mhm." I pretended to think about this for a moment. "You could have told a teacher." Exactly the advice I'd been given as a teenager. I hadn't taken it, but there was always a chance that my son was smarter than me. I certainly hoped so.

Jake scrunched his nose up. Okay, so he didn't like that idea.

"I know it's not cool, but it does help," I told him.

"I'm not a tattle-tale."

"It's okay to tell when someone's hurting you."

Jake furrowed his brow and I wasn't sure whether he believed me or not.

"Why are you in so much trouble with this Miles kid anyway?" Maybe if I knew what exactly had happened, I could give better advice. I wasn't ready to give up yet. This was my big parenting moment, after all.

"Because he's mean." Jake pouted.

"What does he do that's so mean?" I was sure Jake hadn't taken his sandwich for no reason.

"He says mean things," Jake said, and then he pressed his lips together as if he didn't want to elaborate.

"Does he call you names?"

"Not me."

"But?"

Jake looked at me with an angry expression. "He says mean things about Daddy! He can't do that!"

*Oh.* It looked like I wasn't the only one worried about what the town's people were saying. But I'd had no idea that their children carried this crap into school with them where it hurt Jake. And that just made me mad. Eli and I had both screwed up in our own ways, but our son was innocent. He didn't deserve this. None of us did, really, but least of all Jake. He was just a kid.

"That is mean," I agreed, rubbing the back of my neck because I wasn't sure what to do about this. I was supposed to impart some sage advice to my child like a true parent, a real dad—but I had nothing.

In truth, I was every bit as angry as Jake was, and that was affecting my ability to think.

"I can't let them talk like that," Jake said.

"I get that." I really did. I felt the same drive to punch everyone who might hurt Eli that Jake did. But I also understood that I couldn't always act on my instincts. And suddenly I knew what I had to tell my son. "I know that you want to protect your daddy. You're an alpha, you know that, right?"

Jake shrugged. "Daddy said so. But I'm not sure what it means."

"It is what you make of it." I remembered getting this talk a long time ago. Not from my dad, because my dad had never had the time, but from one of the teachers at the boarding school I'd visited. I would have preferred getting it from my dad, though. And I was glad I could be here for Jake now.

He looked at me curiously, and I went on. "It's not bad to be an alpha. Some people will tell you that we're aggressive or easily angered and we can't help but get violent." I shook my head. "Don't listen to those people. No matter what happens or what you feel, you're always in control." That had been an important lesson for me to learn. "You didn't have to punch that kid. You could have walked away, if you'd wanted to. In fact, next time, I want you to walk away, just so you know you can. Do you understand that?"

"I can walk away," Jake repeated, but he didn't seem fully convinced yet. "Do I have to walk away?"

"Well, that depends." I leaned in to him. "Do you want to make your daddy sad again?"

He dropped his gaze. "No."

"Good boy." I ruffled his hair again. "So you have to try not to get into fights. No matter what people say. You always choose what you do, and there's always a choice other than violence, okay?"

"Okay," he said without looking at me. "So what's good about being an alpha?"

"There's lots of good things!" I gave him a smile. "You know the reason we so often get into fights?"

He looked at me and shook his head.

"It's because we have so much energy," I told

him. "And that's a good thing, if we use it in the right way. We get things done. We protect the people we love. When a group of people needs a leader, they look to us. We're the ones who take charge in an emergency."

Jake's eyes grew wide. "Like heroes."

Not exactly what I'd been trying to say, but if he liked that idea then yeah, sure, why not? "Exactly like heroes."

He grinned. "I want to be a hero."

"Yeah? If you could pick a super power, what would it be?"

He tilted his head, face screwed up in thought. "I want to be invincible. So daddy wouldn't have to worry about me."

It was official. I had the most adorable kid.

"That would be good," I said. "But I think he's always going to worry about you, regardless." And as I said that I realized that it was true. Because I already felt the same way.

"Daddy's an omega, right?" Jake asked.

"That's correct."

"What does that mean?"

I scratched my head. Did he know how babies were made? Should I tell him? Probably not. He was too young for that. And I could just so imagine what Eli would say to me if he heard I'd gone into biology with Jake.

"Do you know?" Jake prompted when I didn't say anything for too long.

"Well," I started. "I do know. I'm just trying to find the right words. Omegas are... a bit different from alphas, but they're necessary to us."

"A lot of people say a lot of mean things about omegas."

"I told you not to listen to people saying stupid things about alphas. You can't listen to people saying stupid things about omegas either. They're not getting it right."

Jake nodded. "I know. They're mean."

"Right." I patted him on the back. "Omegas are..." *The best partners you could wish for, and if you're lucky, you'll meet one and fall in love with him... and you won't be as stupid as your dad about it.* "They're nurturing and caring. You know, we alphas, we charge head-first into situations, and the omegas are the ones who pick up the pieces when we crash. People who say they're useless don't know what they're talking about. In my opinion, the world needs a lot more omegas."

"Then we have to protect them," Jake concluded, determination shining in his eyes. And I couldn't have been prouder.

"Yes, you got it. But... not with your fist, okay? Your daddy is an omega, but he's also your father, and an adult. He can take care of himself. He doesn't want you to get in trouble to protect him. Do you understand?"

Jake folded his arms in front of his chest and tilted his head again. "Maybe."

"Protecting your family is important," I told him. "But you have to think about what *they* want too. Your daddy doesn't want you to hit anyone, and you have to respect that."

Jake huffed, and then he jumped off the bed. "Okay. I'll go apologize."

He left the room without another look back. I took a deep breath and exhaled. Maybe I could do this parenting thing after all.

# Matthew

I stayed at Eli's place until after Jake's bed time that night. After all, I had some things to discuss with him that we couldn't talk about while the little one was up.

"You did really well with him today," Eli said as he came back into the living room after putting our son to bed.

I felt my lips tug up. "Beginner's luck."

Eli smiled back at me. "Thank you."

"What are you thanking me for?" I asked as he sat next to me on the couch, leaving only an inch of space between us. An inch *too much*, in my opinion. Especially when I inhaled and caught his sweet scent in the air. I wondered if that would ever stop driving me crazy—which, by the way, it never did.

"Being here," Eli said. "Talking to Jake."

I shrugged. "That's easy. I care about Jake. He's a great kid."

"Of course he is," Eli said, finally inching closer to rest his head on my shoulder. "He's ours."

"He really is. He has your smile." And what a great feature that was.

Eli chuckled. "And your determination. He reminds me of you a lot. That used to make me feel odd, you know? I mean... I like that he's got so much from you, but at the same time, it's always made me miss you. And I felt like I shouldn't still be missing a guy after so many years, but the truth is..." He paused to bite his lower lip. Whatever he wanted to say wasn't easy for him to admit. "The truth is that I never really got over you."

I put my arm around him and kissed his forehead. "I never really got over you either."

"I still can't believe you're back."

"I still can't believe I'm a dad."

"Touché."

I licked my lips. "You know, I've been told some things today. About the rumors flying around in town."

"Oh. Yeah. I don't care about those. The only reason I care about them is because they hurt Jake. That's all on me."

"No, it isn't." I rubbed his shoulder. "They're children. If it wasn't for the rumors, they'd find other reasons to be mean to each other. Jake's a smart kid. He'll learn not to listen to that crap. And people will latch on to some other topic soon enough. In fact, I think we can speed that process up."

"Oh?" Eli looked intrigued.

I smiled. "We won't be as much fun to talk about when we're not a secret anymore."

Eli's eyebrows shot up. "You want to go public?"

"What do you say I take you to the finest restaurant in town right now?"

"Won't they be booked out?"

"You forget that you're talking to the richest bachelor in town."

"Oh, are you a bachelor?"

I leaned in so I could speak into Eli's ear, and feel the shiver that went through him as my breath hit his skin. "Well, I'm not married, but am I taken?"

"I think you might be." Eli ran his hand into my hair and pressed our lips together. One moment, two, then he broke away again. "Are you really serious?"

"You don't think we should? Look, I know you have your reservations, and that I've hurt you before. We've both made mistakes, and yet here we are." I inhaled, trying to get the words right in my head before I could say them, but there were so many of them. So many things we'd always left unsaid between us. "You know, when we first met, I was instantly attracted to you. I couldn't think about anything but how much I wanted you. It was intense. It still is. But I used to think that was *all* it was. Physical. My whole life I'd been warned that one day, I'd run into an omega who would drive me crazy and seduce me."

Eli grimaced. "I know exactly what you've been told."

"I'm sorry." I cupped his face. "But you have

to understand that this was what I believed growing up. So when I met you, I thought I knew exactly what was going on."

"You thought I was trying to seduce you? To get at your money or something?"

"No, no, not like that. My mother would probably have said that, but I never thought you had any ill intent. But I figured what was going on between us was just this alpha-omega connection I'd been told about. Just our bodies reacting to each other. Some chemicals in our brains." I exhaled and dropped my hand, gazing into Eli's eyes. "I was young, and I was stupid, and I wasn't expecting to fall in love."

"You..." Eli looked like he wasn't sure whether or not to believe what he was hearing.

"You didn't know that I loved you?"

Eli licked his lips. "You didn't say."

"No, because I was stupid. Thing is, I didn't *realize*. Not until after. When I was already married and Danielle... just couldn't measure up to you. Nobody could."

"I...didn't know you felt that way."

"No." I ran my hand into his hair, playing with a single strand. "You couldn't have known."

He shook his head ever so slightly. "I just wish I had."

"I know. I wish I could go back and do things differently, but we don't have that choice. All we have is right now, and all I'm wondering is if we could start over. What do you say? Are you willing to give us another chance?"

Eli opened his mouth and closed it again. His eyes searched my face, and I wasn't sure what exactly he was looking for, but then he said just one word. "Yes."

It was all I'd wanted to hear.

I pulled him toward me and crushed our lips together, claiming him as mine. He made a small, appreciative noise and heat rose underneath my skin. Nothing had ever felt so right.

I was completely lost in the moment. We both were.

Until we heard a small voice coming from the direction of the doorway.

"Daddy? What are you doing?"

# Elias

I'd never scrambled away from a man so quickly in my life. Matt and I had had some close calls when we'd first started going out way back when, but holy shit. We'd never been caught red-handed. And now my *son* had seen us. My son who didn't know that he was also Matt's son.

Matt and I stared at each other in horror.

*Deep breath, Eli. Calm down.*

This wasn't so bad, right? Jake didn't know what sex was. He had probably no idea what we'd been doing.

"Daddy, were you kissing Matt?"

So much for that theory.

"We were... uh... "Damn it. Seven years of being a parent had not prepared me for this moment.

"I did kiss your daddy," Matt said before I could finish stumbling my way through a sentence. "What are you doing down here at this hour?"

Deflecting from the topic. Smart. I could see how in some situations, it might be nice not to be the only parent anymore.

"I got thirsty," Jake said, still regarding us through narrowed eyes.

Matt got up from the couch. "I'll get you a glass of water."

Fleeing from the scene. Also smart.

Too bad I didn't get to do that.

Suppressing a sigh, I patted the spot on the couch next to me that Matt had just vacated. "Sit with me."

Jake climbed onto the couch and shot me an expectant look. "Are you and Matt like a couple?" he asked after a moment in which I frantically tried to come up with something to say.

I laid an arm around his shoulder and pulled him against my side. "Would that be a problem?"

"I don't know."

"It's been alright so far, hasn't it? We're having fun together, right?"

"I guess." But he still sounded skeptical. "Do you like him?"

"Do you?"

"I asked first."

I sighed, because I knew I couldn't beat playground logic. "I like him. What do you think? Can we keep him around?"

"Yeah. Maybe." Jake shrugged. "If you like him."

I hugged my kid and kissed the hair on his head.

Matt chose that moment to re-enter the scene with a glass of water. "Still thirsty?"

"Yeah." Jake got up and took the glass from him. He took a sip and then looked up at Matt. "You can be a couple with my daddy."

"Really?" Matt grinned. "I'm glad to hear that, buddy."

Jake gave him a smile. "You're alright."

"And you need to go back to bed, "I joined the conversation. "Finish up your water."

"But I don't have school tomorrow," Jake tried.

"Oh, because you got yourself suspended." Matt playfully boxed Jake in the side. "Nothing to be proud of."

"But I don't have to sleep early when I don't have school," Jake insisted.

"Yeah, well, tonight you do." I took Jake by the hand and led him toward the stairs.

"Whyyy?"

"Because I'm not rewarding bad behavior. Up you go."

"Not fair!" But he went up to his room like a good boy, water glass still in hand.

I exhaled once he vanished from sight. That had gone a lot better than I'd feared. Still... I turned to Matt. "We have to tell him." We couldn't postpone this any longer. That wasn't fair to him.

"I know." Matt ran a hand through his hair. "But how? And when?"

"Tomorrow."

Matt raised an eyebrow at me.

"We've gotta rip that band-aid off," I insisted. "I would have told him even sooner if I'd known you were going to stick around."

"Yeah. Okay," Matt finally agreed. "I just..." His lips tugged up in an uncertain sort of smile that I rarely saw on him. "I'm actually nervous about this."

I sat with him. "I'm nervous too." After all, I hadn't exactly told Jake the truth when he'd asked about his other father before. "Jake never asked many questions, but I basically told him that his other father had left to go on an adventure and he'd never returned." Not the best lie I'd ever told, but it had been enough to satisfy a three-year old.

"An adventure, huh?" Matt scoffed. "I'm not sure running a hotel counts as an adventure. Now *room service* on the other hand, that can be adventurous."

I exhaled. "Jake sees his other dad as some kind of hero. I'm sorry about that. It's my fault. I could have stopped it, but, you know... I figured since he was stuck with me for a parent, he deserved to have one father who wasn't a social outcast, even if that father was totally made up."

"I'm sure Jake doesn't mind having you as a parent, and I'm sure he's smart enough to see he's lucky to have you."

I leaned against Matt. "You really think so?"

"Of course I do." He kissed the side of my head. "I just hope Jake's not too disappointed when he finds out his other dad isn't a hero."

"Yeah, me too, but, you know... a regular dad who'll be here for him is better than any absent hero."

Matt's smile seemed a little more confident now. "I hope you're right about that."

*Yeah, me too.*

# Matthew

The next day, we took Jake to the zoo in the neighboring city. Eli had suggested we have some sort of family day together before we talk to the kid in the evening, and I wasn't opposed. I'd always liked to go to the zoo as a child, and Jake seemed to be enjoying himself too. He'd asked for a hat that looked like a lion, and he wore it proudly while pressing his nose to the terrariums with the snakes.

"These are so cool!" he said, voice filled with awe. Kid seemed to have a thing for reptiles.

Eli took my hand and pressed it. "Thanks for taking us here."

"You don't have to thank me. This is what parents do, right? I'm just glad you got the day off work."

Eli waved dismissively with his free hand. "Let's not talk about work. I'm starting to think I bit off more than I could chew with the whole fashion show thing."

"Oh, you're doing it?"

"Yeah, at the end of next month. You want to come?"

The end of next month. Suddenly I got the feeling that Eli was only asking to see if I'd really still be around by then. I leaned in to give him a quick kiss. "Sure, I'll come. Wouldn't miss it for the world."

Eli smiled at me. He looked so genuinely happy that my heart skipped a beat just seeing him like that and knowing I'd put that smile on his face.

This, more than anything, told me I'd done the right thing by divorcing Danielle.

Jake ran up to us. "Did you see that snake? It's huuuge!"

"Show me," Eli said as our son dragged him to the reptiles.

My phone rang as I watched them go. Caller ID told me that it was my sister on the other end of the line. I grimaced as I took the call. "Hello?"

"Where are you?" she demanded. "You need to come home right now."

"Why? What's going on?" She sounded almost frantic, and that wasn't like her. Something had to be wrong. I pinched the bridge of my nose.

"Father had another heart attack."

*Another*? "What do you mean another heart attack?" I'd never even heard of the first one, but if *that* was what had happened, no wonder everyone was so concerned.

"Will you just come home?" She hung up before giving me a chance to respond. Typical. But in this instance, I didn't even blame her. She was stressed. After all, Father had just had a heart attack.

*Oh God.*

Slowly, that information was really starting to sink in.

"Matt?" Eli shot me a curious look. "Everything alright?"

Oh no. Things were *so* not alright. "My father had a heart attack," I said quietly, so Jake wouldn't hear.

"Oh God." Eli held a hand in front of his mouth. "That's terrible."

"Yeah." I took a deep breath.

"How is he?"

"I don't know. My sister just called. She wants me to come home immediately."

"Of course. You need to go. I'll tell Jake that we're leaving."

"Oh no. You stay." No reason the day had to be ruined for all of us. I got my wallet out of my pocket and opened it. "Here, take a cab home when you're done," I said, handing Eli one of my credit cards.

"That would cost a fortune!"

I shook my head. "I don't care." Money had always been one of the few things not missing from my life. If it could ensure that Eli and Jake got to enjoy their trip to the zoo then there was no better use for it. "I need to go. About Jake, I—"

"Forget about that for now. Just call me after you know more, okay?"

"Yeah, I will."

I only hoped that I would have good news to share.

\* \* \*

Traffic absolutely sucked that day. It took me almost an hour to get to my parent's mansion after leaving the zoo. I found my mother and my sister sitting together in the downstairs living room, but no sight of my father.

"What happened?" I asked, coming in. I hadn't even taken my shoes off.

My mother looked at me, but didn't say anything. I'd never seen her so pale.

"It's just as I told you on the phone," my sister said, turning to me. Her face had lost its color as well, but she seemed to be having a better grip on things than our mother.

"Well, where is he? Did they take him to a hospital? Why aren't we there?" What were we doing sitting around here? How could they take it?

My sister shook her head. "He's not at the hospital." Taking a deep breath, she stood and looked me in the eyes. "There's nothing a hospital could do for him, Matt. He's..."

It was like she couldn't get herself to finish the sentence, but I got a good idea what she was trying to say. But that couldn't be right. I'd walked past my father just this morning and he'd been *fine*.

"No," I said. "He's not..."

My sister pressed her lips together so tightly the skin around her mouth went white. "It happened very quickly and very suddenly."

I looked to my mother, but she had nothing to say. She just sat there, staring at her hands. Had she loved him after all? I couldn't help but wonder. But even if she hadn't, the two of them had been a couple for nearly thirty years. Losing him must have come as a shock to her, no matter whether he'd been the love of her life or not.

"She hasn't said anything since they took him away," my sister informed me. "Honestly, I'm not quite sure what to do, but I'll stay here tonight. My husband's watching the kid."

"Thank you." I tried not to sound surprised at her act of kindness, but didn't quite manage.

"Don't look at me like that," she said. "I'm only doing what I have to do as member of this family. It's my duty to see that all of us are taken care of while Mother is grieving and you... I hope you know what you have to do."

What *did* I have to do? My head felt heavy, and thoughts were slow to form and even harder to process. I'd just heard that my father was dead. I didn't want to come across like a fool to my sister, but I was still in shock while she'd had at least a little time to come to terms with what had happened. Hell, she'd probably even had time to *prepare* herself for the possibility that this might happen, while I'd been left in the dark.

And I couldn't help but wonder what I'd done differently if I'd known.

Would I have spent more time with old man?

My sister poked me in the chest. "Do you know what you have to do?"

I rubbed my face with the heel of my hand. "What do I have to do?"

"Go back to Boston and wrap up your business. Find someone to put in charge of the hotel there, because you're moving back here. You have to take Father's place."

Really? I'd always thought we were competing for that. "Don't you—"

"I don't want the job," she cut me off. "I'm happy with my life the way it is, thank you very much. What I want is for you to keep the company going so it'll still be there when my son is old enough to take over."

So *that* was her endgame.

I took a deep breath. "I need a few minutes to myself," I said, turning to leave the living room.

"Matt," my sister stopped me. "Just please remember that this family doesn't work unless each of us plays their part."

My eyes wandered from her to our mother, who still sat shell-shocked. Suddenly, though, she returned my gaze. She didn't open her mouth, but I felt like she was telling me something with her eyes. *Please do as your sister says.*

* * *

I left the living room feeling like I'd kicked a blind puppy by not responding to either my sister's words or my mother's silent pleas. But I just couldn't think about all this right then. My family expected me to jump right into action and be the strong leader I'd always been told I had to be—and I felt like I was letting them down by needing time to process first.

Was I just a total failure as an alpha?

I was certainly failing to fulfill my family's expectations of me.

I hadn't managed to make my marriage work, and the only child I had was my illegitimate son no one even knew about yet. I wasn't planning to keep Jake a secret forever, but I knew my mother wasn't going to be jumping for joy when she heard of her newest grandchild. I'd wanted to come clean about all of this in the next couple of days. Now I wasn't so sure whether that was a good idea, considering the state my mother was in.

Was my sister right and I was just being selfish by wanting things that had never been in the cards for me?

I didn't know anymore. Maybe yes. Maybe not. It was so difficult to think clearly. I pinched the bridge of my nose, feeling another migraine building in the front of my head.

I inhaled, exhaled, and wondered why the world couldn't go back to being as simple as it had been when I was a teen. I'd known my place in life then—even if I hadn't always loved it.

And then I'd met Eli. He'd made my life more complicated. But it wasn't fair to say that without mentioning that he'd also made it a lot brighter. He'd made me dream in color where I'd only seen black and white before. But still, everything he'd made me want was just that. *Dreams.*

And yet, I would have given a lot to go back to that time. To dreaming.

Before I knew what I was doing, I was calling Eli.

He answered almost immediately, had probably been waiting for my call. "Hey, you. Is everything alright?"

No, no, it wasn't, but hearing the soft cadence of his voice let me breathe a little easier. "He's... passed," I made myself say.

Eli was quiet for a moment, taking this in. "I'm sorry," he said then, and I knew that he meant it, even though he hadn't known my father. Eli was like that, feeling other people's pain like his own. "Is there anything I can do?"

Was there? There was only one thing I could think of, and as soon as I'd thought it, the words had already left my mouth. "Could you stay the night with me? At the cabin, like we used to?" Didn't even have to be the whole night.

Eli hesitated. Of course he did. He had a child to look after and a job to return to in the morning. This was an unreasonable request. "Matt... You know I'd love to, but... No, you know what? We'll do that. I'm going to get Griff to watch Jake. He won't mind. Not in this case, I'm sure."

"Really? That would mean a lot to me."

"Hey, I'm here for you, okay? I just need a little time to get things in order here. Say we'll meet up at the cabin in two hours?"

"Thank you, Eli."

He hung up after telling me not to worry about it. I put the phone back in my pocket, feeling a little bit lighter than I had before. Maybe it was only for a little while, but I couldn't wait to escape from here and lose myself in the omega I loved more than anything in the world.

# Matthew

---

$E$li arrived at the cabin a little later than me, but I didn't mind, grateful that he'd come at all as I listened to the crunch of his shoes over the fallen snow outside. We were lucky the roads had been cleared.

I opened the door to let Eli inside and he brushed some snow out of his hair as he entered. "Oh good, you got a fire going," he said.

I tried to smile at him, but it was hard to get my mouth to move in that position, as if something was weighing down the corners of my lips. "I want you to be comfortable."

"Yeah?" He closed the door behind him and took off his boots. "I thought I was here to make *you* comfortable." That said, he took me by the arm and made me sit on the couch with him, as if he was the alpha and I the omega. That wasn't typical behavior for him, but I didn't mind, because I *needed* someone else to be in charge for just a moment, and somehow, he seemed to sense that. Eli was amazing like that. He'd always had a feel for just the right words to say, just the right things to do to make me feel at ease. I didn't know if that was an omega thing or an Eli thing. I suspected the latter, though, even if Eli himself would have insisted on it being the former. He gave himself too little credit.

"Thank you for being here with me," I said.

"You don't have to thank me," he responded, draping an arm around my shoulders and kissing the side of my face. "We need to support each other if we're going to be a couple. And if we're going to be raising Jake together."

*Jake.* Ugh. I groaned. We were going to tell him about me today, and I'd forgotten all about those plans.

"It's okay," Eli said, as if he could tell what was going through my mind. "We'll talk to him some other time. It's not your fault your father died today."

I took a deep breath, because those words were still difficult to hear. As if the fact that my father had passed away became a little more true every time someone talked about it. "I know it's not my fault, but I feel like... it shouldn't bother me so much. And that thought alone is horrible, but we really weren't that close. It's like..." I closed my eyes for a moment, trying to find the words to describe what was going on inside of me. "It's like I'm mourning what I didn't have, a relationship that *could have been*, but that wasn't. If that makes any sense."

"It makes perfect sense." Eli ran his fingers

154

through my hair in a soothing way. I still had a headache, but his touch was doing wonders for that, the way it always did. "You're regretting that you didn't share a closer bond with your father. There's nothing weird about that."

"Maybe. Yeah." I sighed. "He told me that alphas couldn't raise kids, you know? That we don't have the right instincts, and that's why we need women. Or omegas, I guess." I rested my head in my hands.

Eli stroked the hair in the nape of my neck in a way that made me shiver, even now. "You'll be fine," he said. "I've seen the way you are with Jake. You love that kid, and why wouldn't you? He's the best."

Somehow, with those words, the playful tone of his voice and the absolute trust he placed in me, Eli managed to get a low chuckle out of me. "I do love that kid."

"See? Nothing to worry about."

Oh, there were so many things to worry about. But this omega could make me forget all of them, even if just for a couple of hours, and that was what I wanted tonight. What I needed.

I leaned up to place a kiss on his lips. He welcomed the gesture without reservation. And as I closed my eyes and listened to the crackling of the fire place, feeling the softness of his lips against mine, I did feel transported back in time. We were back where we'd started all those years ago. Only this time, more than ever, I wanted to make Eli mine. I wanted to leave a mark that everyone could see in the morning. So that everyone would know who this omega belonged to. I'd never felt the need to claim as strongly as I did now. It was a bit scary in its intensity, even to me, but even so, I had no inclinations of curbing it.

I was lucky, really, that Eli didn't seem to mind when I dug my fingers into his shoulders and trailed my lips down his neck to graze the sensitive skin there with my teeth. He gave a low sigh and let his head fall back, as if granting me permission. And his skin smelled so sweet. As if calling out to me. There was no way I could have held back. Letting my instincts take over, I sucked at the skin, and I bit. Not deeply enough to draw blood, but deep enough to leave dents.

Eli hissed, and tangled his fingers in my hair, pressing me even closer to himself, as if this was what *he* wanted too. He was too much. Everything I'd ever wanted in a mate, and more than I deserved. Swallowing the emotions welling up in me, I let go of his neck and kissed the spot behind his ear instead.

"I love you so much," I rasped. Another way this day was different from the past. I'd never told him that I loved him back then. I should have, but I didn't.

Eli turned his head to meet my gaze. "Do you?"

"More than I could ever put into words." I pressed my lips to his again, my hands finding their way underneath his sweater and his shirt to skate over his skin. He raised his arms, as if inviting me to rid him of the fabric. An invitation I would never turn down.

Thank God I'd gotten a fire going, because it wasn't long before we'd both lost half our clothes.

"I love you too," Eli whispered, sliding his hand over my naked chest. "From the first time you brought me here... until now. I never stopped. Not truly."

I pressed him into the soft leather of the couch, kissing his chin, his jaw, his neck. "I should never have left you."

"I forgive you," he murmured, reaching out to undo my belt as I straddled his hips, feeling something hard and hot in his pants. The scent of his arousal was strong in the air, mixing with my own as Eli opened my fly.

We didn't waste any more time on words after that. I pulled some lube and a condom out of my pants before discarding them, and then I focused all my attention on stripping the omega beneath me as well.

Eli was handsome even with his clothes on, but there was no sight more beautiful than having him naked and willing before me. His eyes dark, his skin flushed, and his cock straining toward his belly as if asking for touch.

Every time I saw him like this, I fell in love all over again. In love and lust. That same need to possess as before came over me again.

"Turn on your belly," I told him, and as soon as he complied, I kissed his lower back, feeling the flames of desire within myself burn brighter with every whiff of his scent I breathed in. I wanted to have him. But I didn't want to hurt him. Not unnecessarily. So I made myself coat my fingers in lube and prepare him for me. He opened up without a hitch, spreading as well as he could in the little space we had.

"Want you," he said on a sigh as my fingers brushed his warm inner walls. His words were followed by a needy sound he made in the back of his throat—and which translated the height of his desire to me even better. It was a struggle, really, to not just grab his hips at that point and ram into him.

Especially since I got the feeling he wanted me to.

But no. He was trusting me, handing control over to me, and I would not hurt him. I'd promised him that the very first time he'd let me take off his clothes in this very cabin, and I saw no reason to take those words back just because he was more experienced now, or because I was horny as hell.

And so I stretched him with my fingers until he squirmed, trying to rub himself on the leather of the couch. Then I withdrew my fingers and leaned over him, inhaling the sweet smell of his hair, tinged with the scent of his sweat and arousal. "Stop that," I told him, wrapping one hand around his cock and swallowing the moan that escaped him with a quick kiss. "I'll make you come. I'll take care of your needs."

"Please," was all Eli had to say in response.

He didn't have to ask me twice.

I entered him slowly, carefully, but once I was fully sheathed, my control wore thin, and the way Eli bucked up against me didn't help matters. He felt so hot and tight that I had to bite my teeth together to keep from biting *him* again. And then he squeezed around me and I thought *fuck it* and went for it, biting the skin where his shoulder met his neck. He gave a low, appreciative moan, and I wondered why I'd never done this before.

*Because you never wanted to leave marks.*

But tonight, I had no such reservations.

In fact, I wanted nothing more than to leave marks all over him. Really give people something to talk about, if they were going to be talking anyway.

I moved from his neck to his right shoulder blade, then to his left, sucking and nipping at bits of his skin, while I lightly dragged the nails of my free hand down his chest. He bucked his hips again in a wordless plea, and I pumped his cock once or twice until he started writhing, asking for me. He was already so close—I could tell by the way his breath came quick and shallow. He was so stunning when he surrendered to me like this, lost in his lust.

Deciding to put him out of his misery, I started to thrust into him. I didn't bother starting slow either. No, we were both too far gone to be satisfied by that, so I went all out, delivering hard and sharp thrusts to his prostate that had him moan out his pleasure in a way that fueled the flames burning within me as well. Over and over I burrowed myself in him, trying to drag out my release for as long as I could. I didn't want this moment to end. I didn't want to face reality again.

But Eli felt too good for me to last long. The moment I felt him come in my hand, making a noise halfway between a sob and a moan, I was gone as well. He contracted around me, as if to draw out all of my seed, and I could have cried with the relief of my release. It wasn't just the force of my orgasm that shook me—although that was overwhelming in itself—it was also how good it was to be with Eli like this. Like lovers who didn't have anything to fear from being caught.

I collapsed on top of him, simply breathing for a moment, and listening to him breathe as well.

"Feel better?" Eli asked after a minute, a lazy smile on his face.

I gave him a kiss. "Much better."

I'd wanted to go back to the past tonight, and I hadn't quite managed to do that, but maybe what we had now was better. I wanted to hold on to it, even if that meant being an awful son. That much I knew.

But even so, there were still things I had to do in the wake of my father's passing. My sister was right; I had to step up and be a leader. I wasn't going to marry a woman of my mother's choosing, no, but I was going to move back here and take over the business. I didn't mind that so much. Being the head of the company was all I'd aspired to be since I was a kid, and moving back here meant being closer to Eli and Jake. The part I minded was the in-between.

I rolled off Eli so we could both get into a

more comfortable position where I wasn't crushing him.

"I have to leave for a bit," I told him then.

"Now?"

"Not now, but tomorrow." I stroked some damp hair back from my face, sitting up on the couch and pulling Eli against my side. "I have to go back to Boston and transfer the hotel I've been in charge of to someone else."

"Does that mean...?"

"I'm moving back here, yes."

"But that's great." Eli leaned on me. "I'd love if you came back here. Means we can spend more time together."

"Yeah." I took his hand and kissed his fingers. "But it might take a few weeks before everything is settled. And we haven't even told Jake yet."

"I told you not to worry about that. We'll figure things out. We can take care of this when you come back."

"Okay. If you say so."

I only hoped he was right.

# Elias

We ended up spending the whole night and most of the next day at the cabin. I'd taken the day off work, knowing full well that I'd catch shit over it, but not giving a damn. I was preparing the charity event mostly on my own, they could manage without me for one day while I took care of my grieving boyfriend. Which turned out to be not all that difficult, really. Apparently Matt's preferred way of grieving was having a ton of sex. I could provide that—happily. Especially when it felt as great as it did that night in the cabin.

Sex between me and Matt had always been sizzling, but now I felt like we'd added a new layer to it somehow that made it even better. More intimate, in a way.

And I loved all those marks he'd left on me, even if they made me feel a little bit awkward as we left the cabin the following day and stepped out into the sun. I considered wearing a big scarf to cover up, but then I caught Matt's eyes lingering on a mark he'd left on the side of my neck, and there was so much heat in his gaze that I decided not to.

There would be questions, yes, but nobody could force me to respond. I got the feeling that Matt wanted to let the world know that we were an item now, and I wanted that too. But our official announcement would have to wait. At least until after we'd told Jake the full truth about everything.

Otherwise the rumors flying around could well hit on the truth before he heard it from us.

"Thanks again for last night," Matt said as we walked out to our cars.

I gave him a small smile. "It was my pleasure. How soon do you have to leave town?"

"It's probably best I go as soon as possible. The earlier I get there, the earlier I'll be back, and..." He shook his head. "Really don't want to stay at the mansion any longer."

"Yeah, I get that. No offense, but your family..." I shook my head.

"They can be a little difficult, but they're not all bad. They just have very strong opinions about how the world works."

"You mean they have outdated opinions about how the world works."

He sighed. "True. They're still my family, though."

"I know." Like I could ever forget. If those people weren't Matt's family, he and I would have had a lot less trouble. "Do you want to come with me get Jake from school? You could say goodbye, since you won't be around for a while."

"Great idea. We could go for ice cream before I have to leave. Or in this weather, maybe waffles or something."

"I'm sure he'd love that." I felt the corners of my lips tug up. I didn't often take Jake out for treats. We simply didn't have the money, but that wasn't an issue for Matt. He could have bought the ice cream parlor, if he'd wanted to. I hoped he wouldn't start trying to spoil Jake, but the occasional treat was fine.

We got into my car and drove out of the woods. Slowly, because a bit of snow had gathered on the roads. It wasn't super bad, but plows didn't come through here as often. The situation got a little better as we made our way back to civilization.

We made it to the school about ten minutes before classes were over, and I spotted my brother standing by the gates. "Hey, Griff!"

"Oh, hi, you two." He turned to us. "I wasn't sure whether you'd be back in time."

"I'm sorry. I should have called you."

He waved me off. "It's fine."

I was really lucky I had such an understanding brother. And as I took in the half-hidden looks some of the other parents were giving us, I wished everybody could be a little more like him.

I turned to Matt. "You remember my brother Griff?"

He squinted. "I don't believe we've been introduced, but I've heard stories."

Oh, right. We'd never done the whole *meet*

*the family* thing. Something else we needed to talk about if we were going to move forward with this relationship. Something else that needed to wait until after Matt had moved back here. I suppressed a sigh while Matt and my brother shook hands.

"Good stories?" Griff asked.

"Mostly!" Matt confirmed.

Griff's eyes twinkled. "I've heard stories too."

"Griff!" I cut him off. Matt didn't need to know that I told my brother *everything*.

"It's fine," Matt said with a chuckle. "Look, there's our kid." He pointed at Jake, coming out of the school. That was indeed our kid. And our kid looked grumpy. I could tell by the way he hunched his shoulders. Was it because I'd spent the night away from home? No, couldn't be. I'd explained to him, and he'd told me it was fine. Especially after I'd allowed him to order pizza for dinner.

Maybe he'd gotten into trouble with some of the other boys again. Sadly, that was always a possibility. Couldn't be too bad, though, if I hadn't been called.

"Hey, kiddo," I greeted him as he stomped up to us.

He looked up at me out of narrowed eyes, ignoring both Matt and Griff. "Is it true what they say?" he demanded.

"Uh... I don't know. What do they say?" I lowered my voice a little to encourage Jake to do the same. I didn't want the other parents to stare. They all loved drama way too much. Especially other people's drama.

He ignored my silent plea for discretion. Scrunching his face up, he turned to Matt. "They say you're paying Daddy to do stuff with you. They say you must be my dad."

*Shit*. We were too late. We'd waited too long to talk to Jake, and now the rumors had reached him first. I looked to Matt, who seemed just as lost as me. After a minute, he managed to speak, though. "I'm not paying your Daddy for anything."

So that was the part he wanted to address, huh? I took a deep breath and took Jake by the arm. "This is really something we should talk about in the car."

"I don't wanna go in the car! I wanna walk!" He broke free from me and grabbed Griff's hand. I cringed. This was a bad temper tantrum waiting to happen. And one that I didn't want to happen in public.

"Okay," I said. "Why don't you and Uncle Griff go home and we'll meet you there?" And once I'd said that I looked at Griff and mouthed *go*. Then I dragged Matt back into the car with me.

"You're just gonna let him go like that?" he asked.

"I'd rather deal with this at home. Too much of an audience here."

"How *are* we going to deal with this?" Matt asked, fastening his seat belt.

"Honestly? I don't know. Seems like he's going to be mad either way, but..." I looked Matt in the eyes. "You have to remember that he's mad because of the way he found out, and because this is confusing to him. He's just a boy, it's not weird if he doesn't know how to handle this. That doesn't mean he doesn't like you or anything."

"I know." Matt rubbed his temples. "God, why do there have to be so many gossips in this town?"

"They're just bored." I fastened my own seat belt and started the car. I wasn't looking forward to getting home, but we couldn't drag the inevitable out forever either.

It was time to face the music and own up to what we'd done.

\* \* \*

We reached the house a few minutes before Griff and Jake came in. Griff gave us a helpless shrug while Jake tried to march up to his room. I stopped him on the stairs. "Jake. Wait. We have to talk."

"I don't wanna talk!" He looked at me with all the fury of a seven year old alpha. "Is he my dad?" He pointed at Matt, disregarding his own claim that he didn't want to talk.

I took a deep breath, regarding my little boy and wishing that I could tell him something different. But I couldn't. "Yes, he is."

Jake stared at me as if he couldn't believe that I wasn't denying this. "You told me my dad was a hero! That he was out on adventures!"

"I'm sorry." It was all I could think to say, faced with my son's rage. I deserved this, and if screaming at me was going to make Jake feel better, I was going to let him scream it out. This wasn't

how I'd planned this conversation to go, but life
didn't often care for my plans.

Unfortunately, screaming wasn't all Jake had
in mind. He stomped down the stairs, walked up to
Matt and stood on his toes as if to make himself
bigger. Then he drummed on Matt's chest with his
little fists. "You made my daddy sad!"

What?

Of all the reactions I'd expected Jake to have,
this wasn't it. And I wasn't sure how to deal with it.

Matt grabbed Jake's fists and held them in his
hands easily. Jake might be a fierce little alpha for
his age, but he couldn't quite take it up with a
grown one yet. "I know," Matt said, kneeling to be
on eye-level with the kid. "I'm so sorry about that.
But I didn't know you existed. I would have come
back for you. Can you forgive me?"

"No! I hate you!" Jake pulled his hands out of
Matt's grip and ran back up the stairs, past me, and
into his room.

I didn't try to go after him.

Matt looked like he wanted to, but I stopped
him. "Let him calm down. This is a lot for him to
take in right now."

"You're probably right." Matt sighed and ran
a hand through his hair. "You think he really hates
me?"

"No." I walked down the stairs. "Don't listen
to that. He told me that he hated me just a week
ago. Kids are like that. They say hurtful things
without meaning them because their emotions get
the better of them. He doesn't hate you, he's just

angry. And he has every right to be, you know? We lied to him. And we probably made him look stupid at school too."

"Yeah, I get it. It's just hard." His eyes wandered in the direction of the stairs and I knew exactly what he was thinking.

"You won't achieve anything by going up there right now."

"But—"

"Please trust me on this. I know him better than you do."

"Only because I wasn't given the chance to know him until recently."

Ouch. The hurt must have registered on my face, because Matt immediately apologized.

"I'm sorry," he said. "I'm just frustrated. I guess I'm acting like a kid now too."

"It's okay. You're right. I didn't give you a chance to know him. But you will. You'll have so much time with him once you've moved back here."

"Maybe I should postpone the whole moving thing. I feel like I shouldn't leave right now. Not with the way things are."

"No, it's fine." I ran my hands down his arms in what I hoped was a comforting gesture. "He needs time to digest this anyway. I'll talk to him. I promise things are going to look better by the time you come back."

He closed his eyes and took a deep breath and I could almost detect his frustration in his scent. My alpha didn't like being passive, but I hoped he could trust me in this. "Okay," he said finally. "I'll go."

"Thank you." I threw my arms around his neck and kissed him, knowing just how difficult this was for him. That he was willing to follow my lead meant a lot to me.

"I'll call you tonight."

"Looking forward to it." For a second there I'd been so relieved to hear he was going that I'd forgotten all about how much I was going to miss him while he was gone. But then he pulled me in for another kiss. A deep, long kiss that made me regret that we had to part.

Until my brother told us to get a room.

I'd kind of forgotten that he was still there, and I broke from Matt with a blush on my face. "Shut up, you," I told Griff.

He poked his tongue out at me, but stayed silent until Matt and I had said our goodbyes to each other. Then he wandered up to me and inspected my neck with raised eyebrows. "Looks like you had a good time last night."

"What? No!" I covered my neck with my hand, then broke down. "Okay, yeah, I had a good time."

Griff laughed, and I had to join in. It felt good to release some tension after everything that had just happened.

"Thank you for taking care of Jake last night," I said.

"It's no big deal." Griff quieted down. "Do you really think you can fix all this?"

I sighed. "I'll have to try, won't I?"

Oceanport Omegas

# Elias

I didn't try to talk to Jake immediately after Matt was gone. In fact, I left him in peace until the evening, when I prepared his favorite food to try and tempt him out of his room. Chili dogs. He'd never been able to resist those, and he was going to be hungry too. My stubborn little alpha had spent four hours in his room.

Fiona gave me a hopeful look too, and I slipped her half a sausage before taking a plate of dinner upstairs.

"Leave me alone," Jake said when I knocked on his door.

"I have chili dogs."

Apparently that was the code word to get this door opened, because as soon as I'd spoken, I heard the shuffling of feet as Jake came closer to me. "I'm not allowed to eat in my room."

"Today's special."

"It's not my birthday."

Did he have to argue with me over

172

everything? "Do you want chili dogs, or not?"

He took a moment to think, and then the door opened just a tiny slit. Jake poked his nose through and sniffed. "You really made chili dogs!" He opened the door farther and snatched the plate from me in the blink of an eye.

If only everything could be solved with chili dogs.

Jake retreated inside his room again, but he didn't close the door behind him, so I followed. For a minute or two, I simply leaned on his desk and watched him wolf down his dinner. He sat on his bed to do so, and I found myself hoping he wouldn't give me a reason to change the sheets today.

*You have bigger things than housekeeping to worry about right now.*

"I'm still mad at you," Jake said, as if to provide confirmation to the voice in my head.

"I know, sweetie." But at least he was talking to me now. That was a step in the right direction. "Do you want to tell me why you're mad?" I knew of course, but I thought it might help him to put his feelings into words.

"I'm mad because you lied to me!" he told me while munching angrily on a piece of sausage. "And now everyone at school thinks I'm stupid because I didn't know!"

Sometimes I hated those kids my son went to school with. Them and their gossipy parents. "Nobody knew. Nobody but me and Matt. The kids at your school didn't know, they only guessed." I sighed. "They were lucky to be right, that's all."

173

Jake put his plate aside. "But why didn't I know?" he demanded.

"We were going to tell you." I sat on the bed with Jake, keeping a few inches of space between us, because I knew my kid, and I knew that if he wanted a hug, he was going to be the one to initiate it. Didn't matter how much *I* wanted to hug him. "I was just... worried how you were going to take it. I told you so many things that weren't true."

"Why did you do that?"

"Just..." I shook my head at myself. How was I going to say this? Ever since Matt left earlier, I'd spent all day thinking about how to have this conversation with Jake, and yet here I was, struggling with the words. "I wanted you to have *someone* to look up to, even if I had to make them up." Would he understand that? He looked at me with eyes slightly narrowed in thought. "You know how people always say these means thing about me? I thought it would help you to know that your other dad wasn't like me. I wanted that for you. I wanted you to have a really cool dad."

"Because people are mean to you?"

I nodded. "I thought you deserved another parent who was a hero."

He tilted his head, looking at me. "But I have you and Uncle Griff. I don't need another parent." And then, as I'd hoped he would at some point, he crawled into my lap and put his arms around my neck. "I hate the mean people."

*Aww.* "Me too, sweetie." I hugged him to myself like he was the most precious thing in the world—which he *was*. "I'm so sorry."

He was quiet for a moment, then he leaned back and asked, "Can I have ice cream?"

"Ice cream?" I raised an eye brow at him.

"Because you're sorry and I'm sad."

Oh, he was definitely going to be a handful when he grew up. "You haven't finished your chili dogs."

"But today's special.'

He got me there. "Okay. You can have ice cream if you'll come down with me."

His eyes lit up. "Okay!"

"But first we have to finish talking."

"About what?"

"About your other dad."

He jumped off my lap. "I don't need another dad. C'mon, let's get the ice cream!" And before I could even argue, he was out the door. "Uncle Griff!" I heard him calling on his way downstairs. "Daddy said I could have ice cream! You want ice cream too?"

I sighed to myself. It seemed this was long from over.

\* \* \*

As promised, Matt gave me a call that evening. His timing was good too—I'd just put Jake to sleep. Not an easy feat, considering the boy had had way too much sugar.

"Hey there," Matt greeted me as I answered the phone, and the sound of his voice washed some of the troubles of the day away.

"Hey, you. You back in Boston?"

"Yeah. Actually, I should probably tell you that I ran into my ex-wife up here."

What? His ex-wife... I remembered her. And just hearing her name filled me with cold dread. "How did you run into her?"

"It's nothing you need to worry about, okay? She came over to get some of her things from the house, and since I wasn't here, she decided to use the place for a few days while she finished some business in town. I guess she's in much the same position I am. Trying to move back to her home town."

"She's staying with you?" That was all I took away from what he'd just said.

"Eli, please. Don't worry about it. I'm only telling you because I'm tired of secrecy, and there's nothing to hide here."

"I'm not worrying," I lied as I started pacing the living room.

"You know I never loved her, right?"

*Didn't stop you from marrying her.* I bit my lip, mostly because I couldn't think of anything to say that didn't sound passive-aggressive. "How would I know?" I found myself asking in the end, because really. He'd left me to marry this woman. And that had *hurt*. I still had the cracks on my heart to prove just how much.

"Well, let me tell you again. I married her because I thought that was what I had to do for my family. My parents would never have let me move out and start working as a bachelor. My mother was paranoid that I—"

"That you could meet an omega?" I cut him off. "That you could fall in love with an omega and then break that omega's heart when you married someone else? Oh wait, I bet she wasn't worried about that last part."

"Eli... You know how sorry I am about all that happened in the past. But it's in the past. I thought we agreed that we both screwed up."

"I know." I exhaled and let myself fall on the couch. "I've just had a rough day. And I don't like the idea of you being with her while I'm missing you."

"She won't be here for long. I promise. I miss you too."

"That's good to know." Slowly, my heart rate returned to normal. Maybe his ex-wife being there really wasn't a big deal. I had to trust him, right?

"So you had a rough day after I left?"

"Well, you know the situation you left me in."

"Yeah, do you still think it was a good idea to make me leave?"

"Oh, I stand by that." I brushed some hair back from my face, thinking about the conversation I'd had with our son. And what he'd said about not needing another dad. I knew he would probably change his mind with some gentle nudging, but for now, that was what he thought.

"Jake still mad at us?"

"I got him to talk to me, but he really is going to need some time to process all this. Right now he's not ecstatic at the idea of having another parent. But you have to understand what a big and sudden change this is for him."

"I know," he said, but he couldn't hide *all* of his exasperation from his voice. "Well, if he needs time, he can have it. I'll be stuck here for a few weeks at least."

"I'll get him to give you a chance when you come back," I promised. How exactly I was going to do that, I didn't know yet, but I would try.

I wanted us to be a family.

# Matthew

Danielle came strolling into the living room almost as soon as I was done talking to Eli. It had been a long call, and I wondered whether she'd been waiting for me to finish.

"I'm sorry," she said. "But I couldn't help but overhear some parts of your conversation. Is it really okay for me to be here?"

Oh, had she heard me assure Eli that I'd never loved her? Inwardly, I cringed. She must have known that our marriage had never been one based on love, and I'd never told her that I loved her, but I hadn't told her that I *didn't* either. "Of course it's okay for you to be here," I said to soften the blow. "I'm sorry for what I said about... us."

"Oh, don't be." She waved me off and sat on the couch with me, a respectable distance between us. "No offense, but you never made me feel you were head over heels for me. One reason we got divorced, remember?" She held up her hand to me to show where her ring had been and now wasn't.

"I know. But I didn't want to be unnecessarily

cruel."

"Please. I fancied you for a while. You're pleasing to look at." She winked at me. "But I never loved you either."

"That's surprisingly good to hear." Maybe I should get her to call Eli and tell him that too. "You know, I'd suggest that we stay friends, but I don't think my boyfriend would appreciate that."

She laughed. "I see you've already moved on. That's good."

"To be honest... I was dating him before we..." I let the sentence hang, and I wasn't sure why I was mentioning any of this to her at all, but I'd had a long day, and it was good to have someone to talk to. There might never have been romantic love between me and Danielle, but I liked her as a person. I trusted her. The number one reason I'd stayed married to her for as long as I had. Aside from my family's expectations and my own screwed up sense of morals, anyway.

"Did you see him while you were married to me?" Danielle asked, one eyebrow slightly arched in that elegant way she had about herself.

I shook my head. "Never while we were married. I can promise you that much. But... up until shortly before our marriage, yes. I was with him."

"I see." She tilted her head a little. "He's not the type your parents would have approved of, I assume?"

I gave her a smile because she got that right. "He's an omega."

She grimaced, but not out of disdain for

omegas, but out of sympathy for me. "That must have been difficult. And you love him the way you never loved me?"

"With all my heart. It feels like he's a piece of me that I'm missing when he's not around." I couldn't think of a better way to describe that hollow feeling I got when we separated. "And what's more, we have a child together."

"A child?" Both of Danielle's eyebrows shot up now, and there was nothing elegant about her expression. I actually felt a little sorry for her, because we'd both wanted children, but it had somehow never happened for us.

"I'm sorry," I said, giving her a look of sympathy. "I'm sure you'll have that with your next boyfriend too." My lips curled up. "I'm sure you'll be an amazing mother." I might have divorced her, but that didn't mean I didn't want all the best for her.

She smiled back at me. "I'm sure you'll make an amazing father too."

"Yeah, I don't know about that." I stroked some hair back from my face. "It's not easy to suddenly be the father of a seven-year old."

"Oh, he's that old already?" She thought for a moment. "Why, he must have been conceived just before our wedding."

"Pretty much. Hey, would you like some coffee? I could use one." I got up to go into the kitchen just one room over. She followed me.

"I wouldn't mind some coffee. So tell me about this son of yours. You didn't know about him

181

while we were married?"

"I had no idea, honestly." I got two mugs out of the cupboards and poured coffee into them. Thankfully, I'd still had some left over from earlier. "His name is Jake. He's an alpha as well."

"Have you told your family about him yet? I'm sure they would appreciate having another alpha to continue the family line."

If only it were that simple... I turned to her, handing her one of the mugs. "He might be an alpha, but he's also an illegitimate child. You know how my mother feels about that."

She accepted the mug from me, and then she shrugged. "So? Legitimize him. You're saying that you love his omega father, so marry him. Make the two of them Lowells."

"It's not that—"

"Not that easy?" She smiled at me. "Darling, you've always had difficulty seeing the simplest solutions. I've heard the news of your father's passing, and while I'm sorry for your loss, it does mean you're going to be the new head of the Lowell family, no?" She laid a hand on my arm. "I know you always wanted that position. It's why you married me. Shh." She held a finger in front of my mouth. "I know it is. And you must know what you could do as head of family."

I could... "I could marry whomever I wanted."

She gave me a grin, letting go of my arm. "Exactly. And you know what else you can do?"

I raised an eyebrow at her. It had been a long two days and I wasn't as quick as I usually was. The fog my father's death had created in my brain hadn't completely dissipated yet. "What else do you think I could do?" Aside from finally being my very own boss.

"C'mon now. You could choose your own heir. And I'm sure if you think about it, you already have someone in mind."

She was right. I could make Jake my heir. With everything else that was going on, the thought hadn't come to me before, but I was sure that with the proper training, he could do a much better job than my bratty nephew.

Oh, my sister was going to *love* this. *Finally* I was going to be one step ahead of her in something.

# Elias

With the shelter charity show only two weeks away, I was busy crocheting little hats for our shelter cats in my living room with both Fiona and Jake helping me. Fiona by resting her head on my lap and Jake by draping threads of yarn around her in order to 'inspire' me. At first he'd claimed that he wanted to learn how to crochet, but he'd quickly become bored of that. He still insisted that he was helping, though.

He *did* get a chuckle out of me, which was nice, although Fiona looked at me as if silently asking me to reign in my offspring, *please*.

Well, okay then. This old dog had suffered enough.

"Jake," I said. "Why don't you make me some drawings of what you think these hats should look like? Could you do that for me? I really don't know what to do."

"I can do that!" He beamed at me, and then he ran to get pens and paper. I heard him smash into something in the hallway, followed by an, "Ooops," and, "I got it!"

"Did you break anything?" I called.

"Nooo!"

I sighed, choosing to believe him for now. Mainly because the dog was still resting on me, and I didn't want to get up.

Jake returned to the room after another minute, proudly holding up his pens. "When I grow up, I'm going to be an artist, like uncle Griff!" he proclaimed.

"Yeah?" I gave him a smile. "That would be nice." Better than what he'd told me the week before. Then, he'd wanted to be a race car driver and I couldn't help but picture my kid in a burning car. Still, I liked that Jake had so many ideas what he wanted to be, and that he was free to choose. I liked that he didn't have a set path to follow. I hadn't managed to go after my dreams, but the same wouldn't happen to my son.

Jake sat on the carpet by the couch table and began sketching out his designs while I continued crocheting. It was nice, really. The only thing missing from the picture was Matt. He still called me every night, but it wasn't the same as him being here. How could it be?

I wanted Matt to be with us.

But before that could happen...

"Jake?"

"Yeah?" He didn't look up from his paper.

"You know, Matt's going to come see the fashion show too." I tried to say it casually and not let any of the tension I was feeling seep into my words, but I didn't quite succeed.

Jake still didn't look up. "Uh-huh," he said and continued drawing. I thought he pressed his pen to the paper a little bit harder, though.

"Could you try to be nice to him when he's there?"

"I don't like him," Jake said simply. Still without looking at me.

I put my hook down and carefully moved the dog's head off my lap so I could stand up from the couch and sit on the carpet with Jake. While doing so, I glanced at his paper. He wasn't really drawing anything anymore. Just making circles in various colors. I hadn't broached the topic of his other father with him since Matt had left nearly two weeks ago, wanting to give him time, but it seemed he was still mad.

That didn't surprise me, not really, but I still needed to do something about it.

"Why don't you like him?" I asked.

"I just don't."

Of course. He wasn't going to make this easy, was he? "Is it because you don't want to have another father?"

He paused. Then he said, "No," and started drawing again. Blue circles now.

I took a deep breath, wondering what to say. This was such a difficult topic. "You two seemed to have fun before," I tried.

He gave me a shrug. "Only because I didn't know then."

"That he was your dad?"

He paused again and put the pen aside. "I didn't know what he did."

"What he did?"

Jake finally turned to look at me. "He made you sad. I hate that."

Right. He'd said something along those lines the day he'd found out. "You think he made me sad?"

"You were always sad when you talked about my other dad."

*Oh.* I hadn't even noticed. I'd always tried to be neutral, if not encouraging, about this topic. I'd never wanted Jake to think his other parent was a bad person—that would have been unfair, both to him and to Matt—but I guess I hadn't managed to keep my emotions completely locked away.

And now I knew why Jake had stopped asking questions too.

"I thought you were sad because he left to be a hero," Jake said. "But Matt isn't a hero. He could have stayed."

And here my lies came back to bite me in the ass. It was time, I supposed, that Jake learned the full truth of what had happened. Since he'd stopped drawing anyway, I put an arm around his shoulders and drew him against me. "It's kind of my fault that he left."

Jake looked up at me with questions written all over his cute face while Fiona snuggled up next to him, clearly wanting to make this a group hug.

"I never told Matt anything about you," I

confessed. "He didn't know you existed until a few weeks ago. If he'd known... He would have stayed." Jake had to understand that he couldn't blame all of this on Matt.

"And then you wouldn't have been sad?"

"Then I wouldn't have been sad," I agreed, kissing the top of my son's head.

"But then why didn't you tell him?" Jake asked in an incredulous tone of voice, like he just couldn't believe how his daddy had missed this obvious solution.

"It's complicated."

Jake groaned. Yeah, I wasn't going to get out of this conversation so easily. He wanted to know everything now. Even the things he was too young to understand. I figured I just had to find a way to put them in *terms* he would understand. "When Matt and I first met each other, we agreed that we would only be together for a few months," I told him.

"Why?" Jake asked.

"Because I wanted to be an animal doctor and he wanted to move away to take on a very good job. That was his dream, you know?"

"The job?"

"Yes, the job." That and eventually taking over the whole company. His family's legacy. What he told me he'd been born to do. It had all been so important to him. I stroked a finger through Jake's hair. "It wasn't only the job, though. He'd also promised to marry this woman before he met me."

"What woman?"

*The woman his parents had picked for him.* "A very lovely lady. When our time together ended, Matt married her, as he had promised. And then I found out that I was pregnant with you."

"I was in your belly?"

"Yes."

"And you didn't tell him about me?"

"I didn't." I should have, but I didn't.

"Because he married that woman?"

"Yes." That wasn't all of it, of course, but I wasn't going to tell my seven-year old son all about how I hadn't wanted to be the family-wrecking omega society had warned me I would be. Or that I'd been too heartbroken to think straight. Scared too. And angry. Jake didn't need to know about that. He didn't need to know that I'd stared at that first pregnancy test in abject horror for what felt like *hours*. Or that I'd taken five more hoping they'd turn out negative.

"You're not angry at Matt because he married that woman?" Jake asked.

"I'm not angry." At least, I wasn't angry *now*. "You don't have to be angry at him either. We've both made mistakes, but we've forgiven each other."

Jake looked at his paper with all the circles on it. "I don't want him to make you sad again."

"That's okay, sweetie. He won't. You don't have to worry about that. He's your dad, and I want you two to get to know each other. That would make me very happy."

"Really?"

"Yes, really." I pulled Jake into my lap and kissed his forehead. "Will you try to give him a chance?"

He sighed and looked up to me. "Can I have more ice cream?"

I snorted, because my kid was too ridiculous. Was I really going to bribe him with ice cream on something so important? "Okay, you can have ice cream."

Apparently yes.

# Matthew

I'd spent three weeks away from Oceanport when things started to look up for me. I'd finally found someone to run the show over here, and I was feeling good about the future of my company as well as my own—when my phone rang and I saw my sister's name as the caller ID.

What could she want?

We'd talked extensively about my move back to Oceanport just two days ago and I hadn't expected to hear from her again so soon.

"Hello, Matt," she greeted me, and the tone of her voice let me know there was something she wasn't pleased with. I still had no idea what that was, though.

"Hi, Karen. Is something the matter?"

"I don't know," she said with an air of derision, "*is* something the matter? Why don't you tell me?"

"What are you talking about?" Sometimes I wished my family valued straight talk a little more.

The Omega's Secret Baby

But no, we always had to perform intricate dances around each other.

"Oh, it's just that I went downtown today and I heard some interesting things about you from my hairdresser. Did you know? You're the talk of the town." She gave a high pitched laugh that didn't sound amused.

*Oh, that.* "You know people love to talk."

"They certainly do, brother. But do you know what they're saying?"

I sat on my couch and suppressed a sigh. "I'm sure you're going to enlighten me in a second."

She laughed again, but her laughter still had a fake quality to it. "They're saying you're seeing one of the town's omegas. Isn't that ridiculous? You must think it's ridiculous, no? Everyone should know you're far too elevated for some small town omega slut."

"He's not a slut," I cut in. Seriously, if there's one thing I could never stand, it's people talking trash about Eli.

"So you admit it." She huffed. "I can't believe you would stoop so low. If you had to go around fucking omegas, why couldn't you do that somewhere else? You know, a little farther away from home where these rumors wouldn't touch your family? It's like you spare us no thought at all!"

I gritted my teeth. "For your information, I don't make a habit of going around and 'fucking omegas' as you so eloquently put it. And I wasn't aware that who I sleep with is any of your concern."

Through the phone, I heard her exhale sharply. "Oh, don't you pretend like it isn't. We belong to an exclusive social class where you have to be careful who you mingle with. You know all that omega wants is our money. Or were you so distracted by your hormones that you forgot everything you've been taught?"

"You're starting to sound like our mother." It was all I could say. My sister was blowing this way out of proportion, just like my mother would. Neither of them would understand that I loved Eli, and that he loved me. Yes, when I'd first met Eli, I'd been a stupid teen and I'd acted on hormones. But so much more had grown out of that. My mother and sister had never had that sort of experience. It was kind of sad, actually, and this conversation was exhausting me. To my family, everything was about money. It wouldn't have surprised me if they'd laced my dad's coffin in dollar notes.

"Somebody has to be the voice of reason," my sister said. "Might as well be me. Promise me you'll stop this foolishness when you come back here."

"I'm not going to promise you any such thing." My love life was *my* business, and I was going to be firm on that. "I'm sorry, Karen, but you don't get a say in who I date."

"You're *dating* him? Oh, please. You can't be that stupid. I've heard about this omega. He's been single for years, rejecting everyone, only to throw himself at the richest bachelor in town? That omega has an agenda. And not a lot of morals. Did you know he doesn't even know who sired his son?"

193

"That would be me," I said, half-wishing I could see the expression on my sister's face. Had to be priceless.

For what felt like a full minute, I heard nothing but her breathing on the other end of the line. I couldn't believe I'd managed to shut up my sister. I finally felt vindicated for all the mean things she'd done to me when we were children. Like that time I fell asleep in the sitting room and she drew stupid things on me just before my dad was having business partners over for dinner.

"I didn't want to believe it," Karen said finally. She sounded almost a bit defeated. "How long has this been going on?"

"We broke it off before I married." And I wasn't even sure why I was telling her this, because it wasn't her business, but at the same time, I didn't want anyone to think that I'd been cheating on my wife. That was not the kind of man I was. "Then we kind of ran into each other again when I came to visit this year."

"Did you know about the kid?" There was a hint of suspicion in Karen's voice that made me wonder what sort of congestions she was brewing up in her head now.

"I did not know," I admitted.

"And he only told you this recently?" She was definitely suspicious. But what of, I couldn't say.

"That is correct."

She sighed. "He's lying."

"He's not lying." There was no way.

"C'mon, why would he keep this hidden from

you for so long when he could have had access to your wealth all this time?"

And of course it all came back to money.

"It's complicated," I told her. "But mostly because he knew that my family would hate the news."

"Is he really telling you that?" She huffed. "What a deceiving little slut, coming on to you now when he knows you're vulnerable and feeding you all these lies."

"They're not lies! And stop calling him a slut!" The nerve of her! I was this close to hanging up.

"Have you seen proof? Because if not, you need to demand it right now!"

I hung up.

# Elias

Three days to go before the charity event and I was starting to feel a little bit queasy. Which took me by surprise really, because I wasn't *that* nervous. At least, I didn't think I was, but this morning, I could barely keep my breakfast down. It was like my stomach wanted to emigrate from my body with all the food it was holding.

And then my cell phone rang just as I wanted to lie down a bit and waste away my Sunday while Jake was watching cartoons.

The caller ID showed Matt's name, and momentarily, the queasy feeling in my stomach was replaced by a happy one, like butterflies erupting into dance inside of me. Drunk butterflies, but still. Only three more days until I got to see him again.

I lay back on the bed and answered the phone. "Hey, you. Everything okay?"

"I'm fine. How are you doing?" After all this time apart, his deep voice went down my spine like a caress.

"I'm... feeling a bit nervous about the upcoming charity thing." Because what else could it be?

"Scrambling to get everything done in time?"

"Nah, actually, I'm mostly done." I *should* be able to lie back and relax, really. But maybe after all of this was over, I could lie back and relax with Matt. I was looking forward to that.

"That's good. I'm excited about the show, and about seeing you again." His voice dropped an octave on the last part of that sentence and gave me shivers.

"Yeah?" I asked. "What are you going to do when you see me again?"

He gave a short laugh, a sexy little rumble. "Rip all your clothes off your body."

"Yeah? And then?" I prompted because that slow built up of arousal within me was keeping the queasiness at bay.

"Take my own clothes off." There was a hint of amusement in his voice, but it vanished as he continued speaking. "And then I'll lie on top of you, skin on skin, tracing the contours of your body with my hands and feeling you shiver underneath me as I suck on your nipples. You're always so sensitive there. I love that. I love the way you moan when I graze you with my teeth just a little."

The picture he painted with his words made my breath hitch. "God, I want you to be here so much right now. I can't wait to feel you on top of me again." I closed my eyes and imagined the weight of his body pressing me into the sheets.

He chuckled. "Are you turned on right now?"

"Like you don't know!" He couldn't say stuff like that and expect me *not* to be turned on.

"Do you have privacy?"

I glanced at the door, which was closed. Griff was downstairs with Jake, and the cartoons would be on for a while longer. They thought I was napping. I could risk it. "I'm in my bedroom and I'm alone."

"Take off your pants." I thought I could hear the smug grin on his face through the telephone.

Oh, this was really happening. Heart thumping loudly, I put the phone on speaker and turned the volume down just a bit so Matt's voice wouldn't be heard outside the room. Then I shrugged my pants off, just in time to hear Matt say: "Your underwear too."

I obliged, happily. The anticipation alone was already making me hard.

"Did you do it?"

"Yes."

"Good. Now lie on your bed and run your hand down to your groin. Imagine that it's my hand. Run those fingers over your balls and along your shaft. Don't go too fast. I like to take my time. Play with you a little. Get you all worked up and begging for action."

Oh, he definitely liked to tease. And it was working too. When I closed my eyes and let his voice wash over me, imagining the hand touching me was his, I had to bite my teeth together to keep from making noise. It was difficult not to go faster than he wanted me to, but instincts kicked in, and my need to please him was greater than my urge to get off.

"Now wrap your hand around yourself."

*Yes.*

I was hard by now, and having my hand—his hand—around me felt so good. I sighed.

"Do you want me to move that hand? Get you off?" Matt was starting to sound a little breathless himself, making me wonder if he had a hand down his pants too, wherever he was. I hoped so.

"Please," I said.

"How much do you want it?"

"So bad." My cock was hot and heavy in my hand and wondering why it wasn't seeing any action.

"Ask me for it."

I swallowed. "Please get me off."

"Start moving that hand. Slowly."

"Yes." Slowly as instructed, I moved my hand up and down the length of my cock, imagining Matt was here, playing with me. Teasing myself just the way he would. "Need more."

"I don't think you're ready for that yet. Ease off your cock and get a finger in yourself."

It was a good thing I wasn't holding the phone anymore, because I would have dropped it.

"Are you doing it?"

"Doing it now." I got my finger wet, reached around, twisted a little and breached myself, rocking back on my finger and wishing I had something bigger to play with. Something like

Matt's cock. "Feels nice. Not as good as you."

"It's my finger, though, and I'm pushing it in and out of you now. Getting you ready. Can you feel it?"

"Feeling it." I did as he instructed, opening myself up a bit, feeling little stabs of desire as I thought of readying myself for Matt. God, I missed him.

"Good. Two fingers now. Really stretch that hole for me."

I moaned as I added another finger, brushing my inner walls and feeling my need rise.

"Just like that," Matt said as though he could see me. "You're doing so well for me."

I only finger-fucked myself harder in response.

"Wrap your other hand around your cock. I'm going to fuck you now. Entering you slowly but forcefully, can you feel it?"

"Yes," I rasped, stroking myself and in time with the fingers working my ass. My fingers couldn't compare to Matt's cock, of course, but my imagination was really going now. I could totally imagine being fucked by Matt. I remembered the way his cock felt entering me, stretching my walls. I gave another low moan, drawing up the memory of how he felt fully sheathed inside of me.

He couldn't come back here fast enough.

"I'm ramming into you, and you feel so good. So tight around me. So hot. I'm pumping your cock because I love the way you squirm and clench around me. I love those sweet little sounds you make as you get close."

I gasped, jerking myself a bit harder.

"Yeah, that's the sound."

I wasn't even embarrassed. He was right; I *was* getting close.

"Tell me when you get there."

"So close." I panted. "Almost..." I pushed my fingers as deep as I could reach. "Almost... Oh God..."

"I pound you harder. Wanting nothing more than to drive you over the edge. Want to kiss your lips and swallow your moans as you come."

His words, and the images they conjured in my mind, took the last bit of my control away from me and I shook as my orgasm tore through me. I moaned too, wishing Matt was here to kiss me as he'd described.

"Did you come?" Matt's voice sounded hoarse.

"Yeah. And now I'm rocking back against you. Clenching my tight ass around you until you're done."

"Jeez, Eli..." Matt made a strangled noise, and I figured I'd made him happy too. The thought put a smile on my lips. Let no one ever say omegas weren't good for anything.

"That was awesome," I said, exhaling. And the most awesome part was how we hadn't been interrupted, honestly.

Matt chuckled. "It *was.* And to think that I called you because my family was pissing me off."

"Your family's pissing you off?" I reached

around for my underwear and pants. Just because we hadn't been interrupted so far didn't mean it was a good idea to keep running around half-naked. In a house with a seven year old alpha, you always had to be prepared for anything.

"Yeah. My sister called me last night because she'd heard the rumors flying around town."

*Oh.* "You mean the rumors about me and my slutty omega ways?"

"Exactly those." He sighed. "I really hate that people are talking about you like that."

"Don't worry about it. Really, it's stopped bothering me," I said as I put my clothes back on. I should probably go down again in a little bit and check how things were with Jake and Griff.

"Well, it bothers *me*," he said with a huff. "But anyway, I tried to make her see that our relationship was none of her business."

"I'm sure she agreed with you on that." My voice dripped with sarcasm. I'd never personally met the other members of Matt's family, but I'd heard enough.

"Oh, absolutely. Or that's what I would say in a perfect world. But anyway, I told her that Jake was mine."

"Really?" My heart rate had slowed down a bit after the orgasm, but now it was picking up again. "How did she react?" And what did I have to do to protect my baby from these people? I'd known that they were going to find out about Jake sooner or later, but Matt acting so quickly took me by surprise.

"Actually very predictably. She thinks you're lying to me."

I exhaled. Of course. Omegas were not to be trusted in their world. "But you know that I'm not lying, don't you?"

His voice grew soft. "Of course I know."

"I'm sorry. All of this talk is just making me paranoid. I need you back here with me."

"I'll be there soon. And you don't need to worry about my family. They'll be under my lead soon, and some things are going to change. They won't be happy about it, but I don't care. They'll have to accept Jake. And you."

"I hope you're right."

"I am right. And I've gotta go now and get things done so I can hurry back to you. I'm looking forward to your show."

"I'm looking forward to seeing you there. I love you."

"Love you too."

I ended the call and looked at my phone, contemplating all that I'd heard. Matt seemed so certain his family would be falling in line behind him. I wasn't so sure, but the cat was out of the bag now, and all I could do was hope for the best.

I hated that.

# Matthew

The day to return to Oceanport had finally come. I got into town deliberately late so I wouldn't have to see my family before I met up with Eli. He was the very first person I wanted to see before taking care of anything else, and I made it to the hall the shelter people had rented just in time. I noticed that not all of the seats were taken, but quite a few were. It looked like they'd managed to draw a bit of a crowd. That was good. From what Eli had told me, they could really use the money.

I hoped this evening went well for him. He'd put so much work in.

I took seat just as the director of the shelter went up on stage to start talking. It looked like Eli wasn't going to get on stage, which was a tad disappointing but not all that surprising. He'd never wanted to be in the spotlight. His creations were, though. Every cat and dog currently looking for a home in our town was shown off wearing something he'd made especially for them, and everything looked so carefully put together. You could really see how much love Eli had for these animals, and that warmed my heart. He was such a good person. And he'd *so* deserved going to school to become a vet. I still couldn't believe he'd given up on that, even though I knew why.

Wondering where Jake was, I scanned the audience looking for him. I couldn't see him, but I thought I saw the back of Griff's head in the front row, and figured that the kid was probably with him. After the show, I was going to have to go up there and ask Jake how he was doing. *And whether he still hates me.* Eli had promised me that he didn't, but I was still uncharacteristically nervous. I wondered if maybe this was what being a parent did to you. If so, not my favorite part of it.

At least I'd thought to bring a present for the kid. Nothing big, because Eli had told me not to spoil him, but I hoped he was going to like it anyway. I'd spent a whole day in various toy shops, annoying the sales people with my indecision on what I should get.

Not my favorite part of being a parent, either.

But if he liked the present, it would be all worth it. That, I was sure of.

I leaned back, trying to enjoy the show as the most adorable poodle walked across the stage in a pink skirt when I heard the ladies next to me start to whisper among each other. It's not that I wanted to listen in on their conversation, but really, they weren't that great at the whispering part.

"Such lovely costumes," the lady right next to

me said.

"Yeah, such a shame they were made by that omega slut, though. The talent is wasted on him."

"True. At least he works with pets, though. Could you imagine if he worked around children?"

The first lady held her hand in front of her mouth. "Dear heavens," she whispered. "You know I feel sorry for that boy of his. The things that poor kid must be seeing!"

Okay. Enough was enough. Hands clenching and unclenching, I turned to the lady in the seat next to mine. "I couldn't help but overhear you calling my partner a slut," I said, making no effort to lower my voice. If these two were going to be embarrassed by having everyone else know what they were discussing, they deserved it. That and so much more. I was so sick of all the gossip.

Several heads turned our way as the lady tried to stammer an apology. It seemed I'd interrupted the event. I stood, feeling all eyes on me. Good, while I had their attention, maybe I could use this time to set some of them straight. "I'm sorry I've disturbed your show. I know a lot of work went into it, and I'm enjoying it immensely. I just couldn't contain my anger when I heard the poor omega who put this show together called quite unfavorable terms. I want to take this opportunity to let everyone know that I will not stand for that. You might all think he doesn't know who his son's father is, but I can assure you that he does. It's me."

I let that sink in for a moment, seeing everyone stare at me. It would have been a lie to say

I didn't feel a little smug.

"That's true!" I heard Jake's voice from the front row. "He's my dad!"

A feeling of pride tugged at my lips and made me smile. "That's right, buddy." I gave everyone else in the hall a cursory glance. "Excuse me, I will now sit down again, because my partner has put a lot of effort into this show. Please do continue to enjoy it." I sat back down while the lady next to me did her very best not to look my way.

*Bitch.*

She had no idea how much Eli had sacrificed to raise Jake, and I was sure it didn't matter to her either, but I wasn't going to let people talk shit anymore. Not in my vicinity, anyway.

All in all, I was feeling pretty good about myself.

Jake had just called me his *dad.*

How amazing was that?

I was a *dad!*

*Holy shit.*

I spent the rest of the show playing with the gift bag I'd brought, trying not to let my nerves get the best of me. At least it seemed like Jake had forgiven me. That was good, right?

And just as soon as the show was over and everybody started vacating their seats, Jake ran up to me, squeezing past the ladies who'd sat next to me and who were about to leave.

"That was awesome!" he said with a big grin on his face. "You stood up for Daddy!" He seemed really excited about that.

207

"Of course." I reached out to ruffle his hair. "I will always stand up for him."

"Then I like you," Jake proclaimed proudly. "You can stay."

"I'm glad." And so relieved. Oh my God. "Actually, I brought you something." I held the bag out to him.

"Really? Cool!" He snatched the bag from me. "What is it?" he asked, even as he dug a gift-wrapped box out of the bag. Quickly, he tore the wrapping off, revealing a box of high-quality coloring pens in some 70 shades. It was the biggest set I could find at the store.

"I got the feeling you liked to draw and color," I said.

"Wow." He stared at the metal case in his hands and opened it. "There's so many! Griff has some like these. But he won't let me use them. He says I break them!"

I smiled. "Well, now you have your own pens." I was tempted to tell him that I was going to buy him new ones if he broke them, but I got the feeling that wouldn't be good parenting and something that Eli would consider *spoiling*.

"Thank you!"

"You're welcome. Hey, listen, you want to come to my place some time, go sledding on that big hill?"

"Can I really?"

"Sure." Just as soon as I'd talked to Eli about this, anyway.

And speaking of the devil...

"Wow, these are very nice," I heard Eli's voice

and looked around to see him behind me. I'd been so busy with Jake I hadn't noticed him approach, but now that he was here, and so close, his presence nearly overwhelmed me after all this time apart. He smelled so nice, so *Eli*. That was something the phone calls couldn't give me. "Did you say thank you?" Eli addressed Jake.

"I did! I love them!" Jake turned to me again. "I'm going to be an artist, you know?"

An artist? I glanced at Eli, but he was just making this face that told me to please be encouraging. I looked at Jake again. "That's nice."

"I'm going to show these to Griff!" Jake ran off with his present.

I released a breath. That was the most difficult part of the evening taken care of.

"So uh... you said a lot of things tonight," Eli said.

"Yeah." I stood from my chair now that Jake was gone. "I'm sorry if that was uncalled for. I'm just fed up with these people."

"No, it was... actually really great. Thank you for standing up for me." The faintest blush colored his cheeks, and he looked lovely like that. I couldn't wait to take him home.

"Somebody has to," I said.

"I can't believe you told everyone."

"Me neither. But I think it's a good thing."

Eli smiled at me. "Yeah?"

"Yeah, because now I get to do this." I leaned in and kissed him, visibly staking my claim for anyone who cared to look. This omega was mine, and anyone who wanted to hurt him had to go through me.

# Elias

———◆———

"That was a really good show," Matt told me as we went out to walk the dog together after the charity event.

"Really? I'm glad you think so. Some of those ideas were Jake's. He might just make a fine fashion designer someday." I laughed. Tonight was a good night. Matt was back with me and the show had been so successful that my boss talked about promoting me. I had other plans, though.

"A fashion designer?" Matt asked. "Is that really what you want for him?"

I shrugged. "He's seven. There's no telling what he's going to be when he grows up, but I wouldn't mind if he went into fashion. I'll support him whatever he wants to do. Won't you?" I stopped to look at Matt while Fiona tugged at the leash. "Be patient, old girl," I muttered. She really never acted like the old dog she was.

"I... just want what's best for him," Matt said eventually.

"And what do you think is best for him,

211

exactly?" I feared that this road would lead us into a fight—and so soon after getting back together!—but I had some suspicions what was going on in Matt's mind, and I had to make sure that we were on the same page parenting-wise.

"Well, you know about my family's multi-million dollar business."

I took a deep breath, because this was exactly what I'd feared. Matt trying to drag Jake into that horrible family of his and their business. "I want Jake to be able to walk his own path in life."

"Being the head of a company like ours will allow him to do that. He'll never have to worry about money."

"No, but he'll work so many hours that he won't have any time to enjoy that money until the stress takes him to an early grave."

One of Matt's eyebrows arched up. "Do you think that's what's going to happen to me?"

"No, because I'll be there to entice you to take some breaks."

"You can be there for our son as well."

"I'm hoping he'll find a partner of his own to keep him in check. And *not* someone we pick for him," I added just in case.

"No argument there," Matt said. "If anyone knows arranged marriages aren't the best way to go, it's me."

"I guess so." I took his hand in my own. "Seriously, though. It's important to me that Jake can be whatever he wants to be. That's what my parents wanted for me, and I..." Really fucked that up. I still remembered the fight I had with my parents when I told them about my pregnancy. It had been absolutely awful. I never got over it until Jake was born and I felt my baby boy wrap his tiny hand around my finger, changing my life and my priorities completely. But Jake didn't need all of my time anymore, and... "You know I'm actually thinking about going back to school. I want to give it another try."

"Really?" Matt gave me the brightest smile in the glow of the street lamps. "That's fantastic! You definitely should. You've always had so much potential." He brushed his lips against mine. "I'm proud of you."

For a second there, I felt so warm I forgot it was still winter. "I'm so happy you feel that way."

"I really do. And I get what you're saying about Jake, but if you want him to have every option open to him, shouldn't taking over the family business also be an option?"

I bit my teeth together because how was I supposed to respond to that? I couldn't argue with that.

"Look," Matt said. "I can tell you're not loving this, but at least give it a chance, okay? Actually, I've asked Jake if he wanted to come sledding at my place, and he seems enthusiastic."

"You want to introduce him to the family?"

"I doubt they'll bother talking to us while we're out there, honestly, but I'd like to get them used to his presence. And Jake has a right to know where he comes from as well."

I cringed, instantly feeling guilty, since so far, it had been me who stood between Jake and the other side of his family. "Fine," I said. "You can take him. Just... make sure he doesn't get hurt."

"You're not coming?"

I shook my head. "You two need to spend some time together by yourselves. And I'm pretty sure your family would freak if they spotted me on their grounds. I don't want to make this any harder on Jake than it's already going to be anyway."

"Okay. I get your point."

My strong alpha looked a teeny bit nervous now. Good. Being nervous would make him careful. I hoped.

# Matthew

---◆○◆---

The Saturday following the charity event, I picked my son up at his house to go sledding with him—and introduce him to the family he'd never known about. To say that I was a little bit nervous would have been an understatement. I needed this day to go well. To that end, I'd spoken to my sister earlier that day. She was still at the house to support Mother—who still seemed out of it most of the time.

"Are you trying to give Mother a heart attack by bringing that bastard child here?" my sister had asked.

"Please," I'd told her. "Look at her. She won't even notice."

"You would never have done this while Father was still around."

"Well, we will never find out, because that isn't the case anymore. Father installed me as his heir and—"

"The only reason you're the heir is because Father never got around to changing his will before

215

he passed!"

I have to admit, that one hurt a little bit. "Be that as it may," I'd said through gritted teeth, "I'm going to be running the show now, and if I want to bring my son around, I will. And if I find that you can't behave nicely around him, that'll have consequences for *your* son's future in the family business."

Karen gasped audibly. "Are you threatening me?"

"I'm warning you." And I'd left it at that, reasonably sure that my sister wouldn't interfere with my plans for the day.

In hindsight, I wasn't wrong, but I might have been a little too optimistic about the whole situation.

Things started off well, though.

I parked my car by the mansion, and almost as soon as I did, Jake undid his seat belt and hopped out.

"This house is so big! You really live here?"

"Yeah, I do," I said, getting out of the car myself. "I grew up here."

"Wow." Jake's mouth was open wide. "You must have a lot of money. You must be like, super rich."

The astonishment in his voice made me smile. "I do okay." Since money had never been an issue to me, seeing my kid so impressed by it was weird to me. But I had to remember that Jake had been raised by a struggling omega. *Who could have come to you for help any time.*

But no point in being bitter about that.

I just had to make the most of the time I had with Jake going forward.

"Can you buy me a car?" Jake asked, snapping me out of my thoughts.

"A car?" I had to laugh because Jake was making starry eyes at me. "What would you be doing with a car?"

"Drive it! Duh!"

"Sorry, you're still too young to drive."

Jake's face fell. "That's lame. I want to drive *now*. And I want a car."

"You'll have to wait, kiddo. But if you're good, I'll get you a car when you're old enough to drive one."

Jake's eyes widened again. "Really?"

"Sure thing. Just... uh, don't tell Daddy about this yet, okay? This is just between us." Because Eli had warned me so much of spoiling him, saying I shouldn't try to buy his love and all that... But seriously, I could give my son a car, right? Not like I was promising him a boat or anything.

"Oh, a secret! Okay! I won't tell. Pinky swear!" Jake held his pinky out to me, and we shook on it. Suddenly I felt like I was part of a secret club, with the only other member being Jake. I actually kind of liked it. Felt like we were finally starting to bond.

"Okay, buddy," I said. "You wanna go sledding?" And then after, I would give him a tour of the house.

"Yeah! Let's go!" He tugged on the sleeve of

217

my coat, and off we went.

The temperatures had been going up a bit lately, but luckily, there was still a good amount of snow on the hills behind the mansion. Enough snow for a fun day with my son.

We went down the biggest hill a couple times, Jake cheering all the way to the bottom and then immediately wanting to go again. He was an energetic kid, but that wasn't bad. Having a lot of energy was good. But I was grateful I'd become a parent at a young age, or I would have had a hell of a time keeping up with him.

In fact, I did have to ask for a break after about an hour of this, even though Jake looked as if he could have gone on forever and I was starting to think that maybe I should buy him a motor sled rather than a car.

But I was sure Eli wouldn't like *that* at all.

Could I keep that a secret too?

Nah, motor sleds were tough to hide.

"You really need a break?" Jake asked, tilting his head.

"Yeah. But just a short one. Hey, I know, why don't we have some hot chocolate? My friend Frederica makes the best hot chocolate."

"I like hot chocolate!"

"Okay, then we'll go get some." I took Jake by the hand and went inside the house with him, turning in the direction of the maids' quarters. Little chance to run into family here. I wanted to introduce Jake to my mother and sister eventually, but maybe not right now. I was way more exciting about Frederica meeting him, anyway. She was going to *love* him.

I knocked on her door and she opened almost immediately. "Well, if it isn't my favorite Lowell!" And then she spotted the kid. "Oh, you're bringing me a little visitor!"

"I am! Frederica, this is my son Jake. Jake, this is Frederica, the best housekeeper in the whole wide world *and* maker of the best hot chocolate."

"Hello, Jake." Frederica greeted my son with a smile. "I guess you want some hot chocolate? Oh, you're covered in snow!" She brushed some flakes off his coat. "Come inside, inside. I'll have you fixed up in no time." She ushered both of us through the door and closed it behind us.

"So, did you introduce him to anyone else yet?" she asked me then.

"I thought you should be the first."

"Oh." She tapped my nose. "Aren't you a good boy? I'll spike your hot chocolate."

"Frederica—"

"Just a little bit." And then she went through her kitchen like a whirlwind while Jake and I sat on her couch.

"Matt?" Jake looked at me with a question on his face.

"Yeah?"

"What do I call you?"

"How do you mean?"

He tilted his head to the side. "I mean, because you're my dad now. Do I have to call you dad?"

"Oh, you don't have to do anything you're not comfortable with. This is still so new, why don't you just keep calling me Matt for a while?"

"But can I call you dad?"

*I can't wait for you to do that, kid.* "Sure. Whenever you're ready."

"Okay." He glanced over to the kitchen, where Frederica was still boiling milk, then back to me. "Can I ask you another question?"

"Certainly. You can ask as many questions as you like."

Jake drew his lower lip between his teeth for a moment. "You're not going to leave Daddy again, are you?"

"Oh, Jake, of course I'm not going to do that!" I was tempted to draw the boy into a hug, but wasn't sure whether or not it was too early for us. Sometimes I still found it difficult to tell how to act around the kid, and part of me wondered whether that was what my father had been referring to. The *instincts* I didn't have.

And before I could come to a decision, the door to Frederica's chambers flew open.

In came my mother.

*Oh my God.*

I only had to see the look on her face to know that this was not going to go well. The woman was *angry*. It was a surprising change from the lethargy she'd been displaying since my father's death, but not a particularly welcome one.

*She knows.*

That much was clear to me in an instance.

Somehow, she'd found out about Jake, and that I'd brought him here.

"Where is he?" my mother demanded, waltzing into the room.

"You can't barge in here like that!" Frederica tried, but she was ignored.

The moment my mother spotted me and Jake, there was no stopping her. "You!" She came up to me and stabbed her finger in my chest. "What are you trying to do? Do you want me to have a heart attack like your father? I can't believe you would do this to this family after all we've done for you! I've never been more disappointed in my life! To think that you would fall into the hands of a greedy omega after all the effort I went through to prevent that from happening!" She put the back of her hand to her forehead in a dramatic gesture.

"Please, Mother. You're over—"

"Don't tell me I'm overreacting!" She stabbed my chest again. "Your sister told me everything! Some dirty omega's got you convinced that you knocked him up eight years ago and now you feel like you have to raise his bastard child. Is that true?" She glanced at Jake, who stared at her with wide eyes. "Is that the bastard child? He looks nothing like you!"

"He has my eyes. And you will stop calling him a bastard!"

"He does not and I will not!"

"Then get out of here! You're scaring the child!"

"You can't tell me what to do in my own

house! And maybe that child needs to be scared so he won't come back!" She turned to Jake. "We don't need the likes of you here!"

I stood and dragged the woman away from my son. She might have been my mother, but there was a limit to the level of abuse I could tolerate. Especially when it was directed at my kid. "That child is my son, and you will treat him with respect!"

She did the most unladylike thing I'd ever seen her do—she spit in my face. "That is not your child. Get him out of my sight!" That said, she turned on her heel and left.

I swallowed, watching her go, balling my hands into fists. I couldn't believe Karen had sicced our mother on me. Well, actually, I *could* believe it. What I couldn't believe was that I hadn't foreseen it. All this time, and I still hadn't learned that basic human decency counted for nothing in this family.

"Matt." Jake tugged on my sleeve. "I want to go home now."

Of course he did. Who could blame him?

"Sure, kiddo." I gave him the hug I'd wanted to give him earlier. "I'll take you."

Well, this had gone wonderfully. I could only hope that Eli wasn't going to rip my head off.

# Elias

———◆◇◆———

Matt brought Jake back a bit earlier than I'd expected. I was in the middle of doing a crossword and trying to enjoy my rare alone time instead of worrying about my kid when the doorbell rang.

Jake greeted me with a hug, which surprised me, because he wasn't doing that as much lately.

"Hey, kid," I said, returning the hug, relieved to have him back with me. "Did you have a good time?"

Jake looked up at me with a curious expression. "Daddy, what's a bastard?"

My heart just about burst into a million pieces. "That's uh... That's a word we don't use. Ever. Okay?"

"But what does it mean?"

"It uh..." I looked at Matt, but he didn't seem to have an appropriate explanation either. Before I knew it, my eyes narrowed at him. How the hell had this happened? I'd let him watch my kid for *one* day! I looked back at Jake. "Go up to your room. We'll talk later."

"But—"

"Go to your room now. Please." I had to talk to Matt, and I wasn't going to do it with Jake present.

Jake huffed, but went up the stairs. I was going to have to console him with some ice cream later.

For now, though... I glared at his dad. "Care to explain to me what happened?"

He exhaled, posture just a little stiff. "Things were fine at first. We were having a lot of fun sledding. Then I took him into the house to meet our lovely housekeeper and have some hot chocolate. I figured we wouldn't run into family in the staff wing, but...well."

"But what?" I'd *told* him to be careful, goddammit.

"My sister had a bone to pick with me and put our mother on my trail."

"And your mother called him..." I didn't even want to repeat that word. Just thinking it made me so mad I wanted to punch something or someone, and I never usually felt that way. I didn't even know how to handle that kind of emotion. I only knew that I had to protect my son from whoever was trying to hurt him.

Alphas weren't the only ones with protective instincts. There was no wrath like the wrath of an omega whose baby had been put into jeopardy.

"My mother said a lot of mean things," Matt admitted.

"*A lot* of mean things?" I demanded.

"Yeah, but you know she's not all there." Matt made a gesture with his hand as if to signal that his mother had gone cuckoo. "She's been a bit off since my father passed away."

"And you took our kid to see this mentally unstable..." I stopped short of saying bitch, but it was a close call.

"I honestly didn't think it was going to be this bad." He held his hands up.

How could he *not* think that? How had *I* not foreseen this? I sort of had, but I'd wanted to trust Matt. Give him a chance to prove to me that I was worrying too much.

*Stupid, stupid, stupid.*

I was so mad at myself it felt like something within me was about to explode, and I turned that on Matt. "You know what your problem is? You were always a privileged kid. A rich alpha on top of the food chain. You know on some level that your family isn't super decent, and I give you credit for that, but you don't *really* know. You don't know what it feels like to face the kind of prejudice Jake and I have to deal with. You know one reason I didn't tell you I was pregnant? Because I knew you weren't equipped to deal with this kind of situation!"

Matt's mouth dropped open but he didn't say anything for a few seconds. "You had no right to judge whether or not I was equipped with any situation!" he finally got out.

"Maybe not," I conceded, "but I'm starting to feel like I made the right call anyway." I knew I was saying the wrong thing, going too far, the moment the words were out of my mouth, but then they hung in the air between us and I couldn't take them back.

Matt only looked at me for a moment. And then he turned and left.

I didn't even blame him.

\* \* \*

After Matt had left, I went up to Jake's room to do some damage repair. Honestly, I felt like most of my time as a parent was spent fixing one problem or another. At least I got a really sweet kid in exchange for all the trouble, though. I wouldn't trade Jake for the world, even if worrying about him kept me up too many nights.

I knocked on his door and stuck my head into his room. Jake was on his bed with a coloring book. "Hey, kiddo," I said, entering the room. "You okay?"

He sat up. "I'm okay," he said cautiously, and I could tell by the look on his face that he *hadn't* gone straight to his room, but he'd heard me and Matt fight. And I had no idea how he felt about that—or any of the things that had happened today.

I sat on the edge of his bed. "I think there's some things we should talk about."

"Yeah?" Jake put his coloring book aside. "Are you going to tell me what a bastard is?"

There was no getting around this, was there? "It's... it's a very mean word for a child whose parents weren't married when he was born."

226

"Oh. So I *am* a bastard."

"No!" I hugged Jake to myself before the seven-year old could protest. "I don't want you to say that again, ever, okay? People only use that word to hurt people they think are beneath them, and you're not beneath anyone. That's an outdated belief."

"Matt's mom said it."

I shook my head. "Matt's mom is not a very nice woman. And she has a lot of outdated beliefs. You can't listen to her."

"I don't think I want to go back there."

"You don't have to, sweetie. Not if you don't want to."

"The sledding was awesome, though."

"That's good." I kissed his hair. "I'm glad you had some fun."

For a moment, we sat in silence, my arm still around Jake. After a minute or so, Jake looked up at me with a serious expression. "Is Matt going to leave again?"

"You heard us fight, didn't you?" I might have raised my voice a little too, on my tirade.

Jake shrugged.

"We only fought a *little*," I said.

"Was it because of me?"

"Hey, whatever happens between Matt and me is not your fault, okay?"

He nodded, even though he didn't seem entirely convinced. Holy hell. I'd *known* this relationship might be tough on him, and yet I'd thrown caution to the wind when Matt kissed me. I just couldn't help myself around him. Even when I was mad at him, I still loved that stupid alpha like there was some sort of magnetic force pulling us together. All these years, and that hadn't changed. It should have changed. I should have grown up.

"Are you and Matt going to make up?" Jake asked.

What to say? I didn't know. Maybe I had screwed up too hard by not telling Matt about Jake eight years ago. Or maybe our worlds were just too different. "I hope so," I said, brushing some hair back from my son's face. "But you know, whatever happens, he'll still come to see you. I know he loves you." Even if he didn't always make the smartest parental decisions.

Matt was right; I should never have kept him away from Jake in the first place. But it was too late to fix that mistake.

* * *

That day, after I'd put Jake to bed, Griff and I spent the remainder of the evening eating ice cream and watching mindless television shows. It was great to have a brother like him in times of crisis. Actually, it was great to have a brother like him, full stop.

"Thanks for staying up with me," I told him, licking some chocolate ice cream off my spoon.

"Don't worry about it." He passed the rest of his ice cream to me. "I'm done with that, if you want it."

"You? Done with ice cream before me?"

"I don't know, man, you seem to be really into that stuff tonight."

I looked at the tub of ice cream I'd nearly completely annihilated and couldn't disagree with him. Usually Griff had a much bigger sweet tooth than I did. The man ate chocolate bars for breakfast, for god's sake. The only time I'd ever out-snacked him was...

*Oh dear God.*

Griff and I looked at each other and I could tell by the look on his face that he was having the same horrifying thought.

My brother spoke first. "Tell me, is it at all possible that you..."

"We used protection." I'd made sure of that! Nobody wanted to repeat past mistakes.

"Did you really?"

"Yeah, man, I keep condoms by my bed."

"How long have you kept them there? Because, no offense, but you don't bring a lot of guys back here."

Hearing my brother's words, a horrible suspicion dawned on me. I stormed up to my room and got the pack of condoms out of my bedside drawer. Then I fumbled with it until I found the expiration date.

It was two years in the past.

*Fuck.*

# Matthew

Eli's words kept ringing in my head as I returned to the mansion. Was I really such a horrible parent? Was it better for Jake if I stayed away from him? Had my father been right after all?

I wanted to slam my hands on the steering wheel in frustration. Goddammit. Things had seemed to be coming together so beautifully. And then that. Part of me thought I should have a talk with my sister. Part of me thought never talking to her again would be the preferable option.

For now, I parked the car and headed back into the house, only to be met by Frederica on my way up to my quarters.

"I thought I'd heard your car," she said with a sympathetic smile. "Rough day today, huh?"

I held a hand up. "Please keep it out of the gossip loop."

"Oh, you know I won't talk about it. So tempting, though. Your mother looked like a wild goose storming into my living room." Frederica laughed just a little and the sound was so contagious that I felt my lips curve up in spite of everything.

"Would you like to have a tea with me?"

"Oh, I think tea is just the thing we need now."

If only all problems could be solved by tea. I led Frederica up to the sitting room in the west wing of the second floor, which was generally considered *my* wing and blissfully devoid of people.

"Green tea?" I asked her, grabbing some cups from the shelves.

"You know how much I love green tea."

"Yeah, I know." Apparently there were still *some* things I got right. I prepared the tea for the both of us and put the mugs onto a coffee table before settling in one of the arm chairs.

"So," Frederica asked. "You take the kid back home to the omega? It's a shame, I must say. I was looking forward to chatting with him. He seemed like a sweet little boy." Her eyes twinkled. "Reminds me a little bit of certain alpha I know when he was young."

"You really think he's like me?"

"A little bit," Frederica said, pinching her thumb and index finger together. "Your mother has no idea what she's talking about. Then again, she was never your primary caretaker." A hint of disdain entered Frederica's voice.

"No, I guess not. Just not the way things are done in this family." Seriously, how had I thought I was going to be a good parent when I had no good example to draw on?

"You'll do things differently now, won't you?" Frederica stirred some milk into her tea.

I raked a hand through my hair. "I'm not sure *what* to do right now, to be honest."

"Had a fight with the omega?"

"His name is Eli," I reminded her, because Eli was so much more than just an omega. "And you just want me to tell you the juicy bits, don't you?"

She grinned. "Caught me. But really," her voice grew more serious, "you can talk to me if you're having trouble."

"Well, we did get into a bit of a fight. I have to admit that this day didn't go as I'd planned, but he... He said some pretty harsh things."

"Are you sure he meant them? In my experience, parents can get a tad irrational when their babies are involved."

"I don't know. He basically said I was a privileged rich kid who couldn't understand the real world. Or at least, the world he lives in, whatever that is." I pinched the bridge of my nose.

"Well, you certainly live in a world different from most people," Frederica said.

"You really think so?" Was I so unaware?

"I'm not saying this to be mean, but life is different for people who have money, people of your standing... That's just the way it is. And your family has always had some strong ideals that are entirely antiquated, and you were raised with them." She shot me a sympathetic look, as if to apologize for what she'd said. "If it helps," she continued, "I've always thought you were the best of the bunch. Honestly, I'm kind of surprised to see you back here."

"How so?" Why would she be surprised to see me here? I'd always wanted to take over the business and be the head of the family. I thought she knew that. I thought she knew *me*.

"You've always been a bit of a free spirit. I've watched you sneak out of the house as soon as you could. You did what your parents asked of you, but I never got the feeling that you really agreed with all of it. Or any of it. I thought you'd eventually pursue another path in life than the one your parents were laying out for you."

"I... never really thought about it that way." Eli had told me that he wanted Jake to be able to go after whatever he wanted, and I'd kind of just brushed him off. My parents had always assumed they knew what was best for me, and I was starting to act exactly like them.

"You know... This might be a bit personal, but I kind of always felt that you were trying to please your father too hard. Broke my heart to see you go ignored so many times."

I squinted, trying to remember what exactly she was talking about. Sure, there had been times when I was a child when I'd wanted to play with my father, but that was only because I didn't know better then. *Oh God.* I rested my head in my hands. Had I really spent my life trying to impress a man who could never give me the time of day?

"I'm sorry," Frederica said. "This must be a difficult topic for you, so soon after his death."

I took a deep breath. For a moment there, I'd completely forgotten that my father had passed away. Was I now trying to impress a dead man by taking over business? Was that what I was doing with my life?

No, that wasn't all I was doing. I had a good job. I *liked* my job. But Frederica had a point. Even after my failed marriage, it was still difficult for me to envision a life that went off the rails my parents had laid down for me.

"What did you think I was going to be?" I asked Frederica. "If not head of this business."

She shrugged. "Whatever you want to be really. You got a good head on your shoulders, an excellent education and all the money you could ever need." She smiled and took a sip of her tea. "Really, sometimes, it's like you don't even know how lucky you are!"

I looked up at her. "I guess I really don't."

"You have a really sweet kid with a man you love. Go and make it right."

"You know what? I will." I stood.

"Hey, I didn't say you don't have to finish your tea first! Don't just leave me here."

I stopped. "Oh, I'm sorry, I—"

She laughed and waved her hand. "Go, go!"

Seriously, this woman... She did have a point, though. I had to go and see if things between me and Eli could be fixed.

# Elias

"Can you go to the drugstore for me?" I asked Griff. I couldn't go myself. The whole town would be talking about my new pregnancy before the day was over. Sending my brother wasn't *much* better, but at least a little better.

"You want me to go buy a pregnancy test for you?" Griff bit his lower lip. He obviously wasn't in love with this idea.

"I'll make it up to you. I just really need to know." Especially now that I remembered the odd nausea I'd been fighting with last week.

Oh God, I couldn't be pregnant again. Not now. Not like this.

*Deep breaths, Eli. Don't panic just yet. Maybe it's nothing.*

Yeah, right. Like I was going to be that lucky. I still remembered when I'd first noticed pregnancy symptoms with Jake. I hadn't wanted it to be true then, either. But that hadn't changed reality.

At least this time I wouldn't have to pee on a stick in a college dorm's bathroom that smelled faintly of vomit.

Yeah, this time was going to be *much* better.

Oh, who was I kidding?

"Okay," Griff said. Maybe he noticed my distress. "I'll go. But you really owe me for this."

"Yeah." I owed him so much already. "I don't know what I'd do without you."

He gave me a small smile. "Anything else you want from the drugstore while I'm there?"

"Any chance you can get Valium there?"

"Probably not. Sorry, man." He patted me on the back and headed out the door.

I took another deep breath and started pacing the living room. What was I going to do about my college aspirations if I was pregnant again? No, no, no, I couldn't think about that now.

I sank onto the couch.

Was I really going to have my dreams smashed *again* by my stupid fertility?

I couldn't do this to Griff again, either. My brother really needed to start his own life at some point. Preferably before he was fifty. I totally owed him too much already. He'd been a godsend through all of this, but I couldn't keep holding him back. The man was still a virgin, for fuck's sake!

*Okay, Eli, breathe.*

Maybe Matt could help me. That was an option now, right? I mean, sure, I'd gotten mad at him earlier, but he was new to this whole parenting thing. It was unfair of me to expect him to be perfect at it from the get-go. Jake was going to survive his run-in with Matt's family, and I'd just have to take a firmer stand on the whole matter in the future. For Jake *and* for this baby. If I was having a baby.

But *if* I was having a baby, could I seriously expect a CEO to spend a lot of time with it? No, his family raised their kids by hiring other people to do that for them. It wasn't generally a bad thing to get a little help, but they were really overdoing it. I was *not* going to hand over my baby like that.

If I *was* having a baby.

Dear Lord, what was taking Griff so long?

I got up and started pacing again. By the time my brother came back from the drugstore, I'd almost walked a pattern into the rug, and not a very pretty one.

"You're back!" I snatched the paper bag he was holding out of his hand.

He grabbed it back from me. "That's my cupcakes!"

"You went to get cupcakes?" While I'd been sitting here worrying? "Where did you even get those?"

"I have my sources." Was he blushing? Where had he *been*? My brother was becoming a mystery to me, lately. I wasn't at all surprised that he had someone to go to for sugary snacks—they were his drugs—but someone who made him blush like that?

*Interesting.*

"Who is he?" I asked.

"No one, okay? Don't look at me like that." He pushed a smaller bag at me that I hadn't seen at first. "Go take your test."

"Okay, okay." If it was important, I'd find out about this guy sooner or later. "Wish me luck."

"Are we wishing for baby or no baby?"

I opened my mouth, the reply I wanted to give on the tip of my tongue, but it wouldn't come out. "Just wish me good luck," I said in the end.

He stepped up to me and squeezed my shoulder. "Good luck, bro!"

I saw him start to dig into his cupcakes as I made my way to the bathroom. God, why hadn't I checked the date on the condoms? Such a stupid mistake!

Closing the door to the bathroom behind myself, I got ready to find out whether those condoms had doomed me to another pregnancy. It wasn't that I never wanted another child, but this *so* wasn't the right time. Not while Matt was taking on new responsibilities and I wanted to go back to school. Not while I wasn't sure if we could even make this relationship work after all. So much had happened between us. So many things left unsaid for too long. Perhaps the worlds we lived in truly were too different.

But none of that mattered if this test turned out to be positive. Then we'd have to find a way to work alongside each other even if only as co-parents. No matter what I'd said earlier, I was never going to repeat the decision I'd made in the past. Keeping Jake from Matt had been a mistake. I knew that. I was just angry. And scared, in a way, of what was going to happen if that horrible family got their hands on him.

The thirty seconds I had to wait for the test result were the *worst*. I was convinced there was some sort of spell on these stupid test sticks that made time slow down while they did their thing.

And then when the thirty seconds were finally up, I couldn't make myself look. Like the chicken I was, I took the test stick and took it downstairs without peeking at the result.

My brother was still in the living room, face full of questions.

I held the stick out to him. "You tell me. I can't look."

"Okay, let me see." He took the stick from me.

I bit my lip and lowered my eyes to the floor. Griff didn't say anything. Why wasn't he saying anything? I raised my eyes again and the look on his face spoke volumes.

*Fuck.*

"I'm pregnant, aren't I?"

"Yeah. Sorry, man."

I took a deep breath. And another one.

I was having another baby.

But I couldn't panic, yet. No, I had to...

Griff stopped me as I turned to leave the room. "Hey, where are you going?"

"I have to call Matt."

# Matthew

It felt weird to sit at my late father's desk. It was a huge mahogany thing that seemed entirely too big, even considering the heaps of documents scattered across it. The room still had this faint smell of tobacco that I always associated with my father, even though no one had smoked in here in a while. Briefly, I entertained the thought of fishing a cigar out of the desk's drawer and lighting up myself, but I'd never smoked, and I wasn't going to start now. Not even in memory of a dead man.

No, I was here to get some work done, if only to distract myself from everything else in my life.

I was looking through some of the papers on the desk when my cell phone rang. Looked like Eli wanted to talk. I found myself hoping that it was to apologize as I answered the call.

"Hey, it's me," Eli said. "I know we were fighting and all, but I've got something important to tell you."

"Yeah?" I leaned forward, propping my

240

elbows on my father's large desk. "Did something happen to Jake?"

"No, Jake's fine. He's asleep." Eli let out a sigh which sounded a little like he was glad children needed to sleep occasionally.

"If it's not Jake, what did you want to talk about? Is this about us? Because I'm sorry about—"

"I'm sorry too," Eli cut me off. "I shouldn't have said what I did. I know what I did was wrong."

"But were you saying the truth? Is that really why you didn't tell me? Because you thought I couldn't handle it? Because you didn't want me to be your child's father?"

Eli didn't respond immediately, which let me know there was at least *some* truth to what he'd said, even if he'd said it in anger.

"Eli? Say something please."

After another moment, he did. "It's more complicated than that," he said. "I mean, yes, you being this high society alpha and me being... me added to my insecurities, but that wasn't all of it." He sounded deflated somehow. "I love you, Matt. I did then and I do now, but there's just some things...Initially I didn't tell you because I was young and stupid and I had myself convinced that I would ruin both our lives. And then over time I also convinced myself that Jake and I wouldn't fit into your world. But that wasn't because I believed you would be a horrible father or anything. I see now that I only did that to reassure myself that I was doing the right thing, even when I knew I wasn't. And I'm so sorry. And I don't know if we can really get past this. I betrayed you."

I wasn't sure where even to start responding to all that. Was this really the kind of conversation we should be having over the phone? "I know you're sorry," I said. "And I love you too." *With all my heart.* "And I think that we should talk in person."

"You're probably right. It's not just that, though. There's something else I need to tell you."

"Something else?"

"Yeah, um... Are you sitting down? You might want to be sitting down for this."

"You're scaring me a little bit," I tried to joke, even though he *was* really making me wonder.

"You remember when we had sex at my place?"

A grin stole its way onto my face. "How could I forget?"

"Well, I understand if you're going to hate me for this, but those condoms we used? Two years past their expiry date."

For a second there, my heart stopped beating. If the condoms were old, that meant they might not have worked. And if they didn't work then... We'd had unprotected sex. "Are you saying what I think you're saying?"

"I just took the test a minute ago. I'm pregnant."

My mouth went dry. I didn't know what to say. What to *feel.* "That's... Wow. We're going to have another child?" A myriad of emotions washed over me like a tsunami. Joy and fear and worry and excitement and love and... so many others that I couldn't even name.

"Yeah," Eli said, voice soft. "We're going to have another child."

"Holy shit."

I heard the smile in Eli's voice as he replied. "That sums it up well."

I laughed. And then I opened the drawer and lit myself a cigar.

*Holy shit,* I couldn't help but repeat in my head.

# Elias

———◆———

$M$att and I agreed to meet in person the next day. We got Griff to watch Jake while Matt finally took me to that fancy restaurant he'd been talking about. Even in my best clothes, I felt way under-dressed as the waiter showed us to our table while classical music played in the background. I didn't have a tailored suit like everyone else here seemed to. *Matt* looked stunning in his, of course. Not that he didn't always look stunning. There was a reason I'd been captivated by this alpha from the moment I'd laid eyes on him—and it wasn't only his smell and the fact that he'd had a puppy in his lap. Looking at him, I could almost forget what had brought us here tonight. Hell, I almost wanted to jump his bones and see if we couldn't make *another* baby.

Better not, though.

*Be cool, Eli, you're in an upscale restaurant.*

"You look really nice tonight," I told Matt as I sat at our table.

"Thanks. So do you." He gave me a smile as

244

he took the seat opposite me.

The waiter handed us our menus and left. I couldn't find any prices listed in mine. "How do you know what anything costs at this place?"

"Don't worry about that," he said. "I've been wanting to take you out like this forever. I don't want you to think about money tonight."

I looked around the restaurant with all its glitz and glamour. The only way it could have screamed *money* any louder would have been if the floors and the plates had been made of gold. "Kind of hard not to think about money in a place like this," I admitted.

Matt reached out over the table and stroked his thumb over the back of my hand. "I'll think of ways to distract you, then." The grin on his face was almost devilish.

It was *so* weird to be out with him like this, in public. Weird, but also kind of nice.

"I don't want us to hide anymore," he said, as if he could read my thoughts.

"No, this is... This is nice. I could just never picture us together in a place like this. I still have to wrap my head around everything that's happened."

"Well, I didn't expect to be the father of two children so soon." Matt squeezed my hand.

"How do you feel about that?" I asked, because I hadn't gotten too much out of him over the phone.

"Honestly? I'm kind of looking forward to it."

His words made me smile in relief. "Yeah?" At least that was good.

"Yeah, the pregnancy, getting to meet this little guy or girl, seeing them grow up. All of it."

"You're looking forward to the pregnancy?" I raised an eyebrow at him.

He grinned again. "Well, if you must know, ever since I found out that you've been pregnant with my child and I missed it, I've been wondering what a pregnant you looks like."

"Fat," I said, laughing. "Seriously, that's what you fantasize about?" Well, at least I didn't have to worry about him leaving me when my body changed.

"Yes, that's what I fantasize about," Matt said with absolutely no shame. "I'm sure you're going to look amazing."

I gave him small smile. "Well, if you think so." I glanced at the menu. "Is it really okay to order anything?"

"Knock yourself out."

My smile grew. "Good. Because you know I'm eating for two now." And pregnancy turned me into an absolute glutton. I ordered at least three things off the menu. The gnocchi, some other pasta dish that I couldn't pronounce and the filet mignon. Matt meanwhile stuck to a simple order of chicken parmigiana and seemed to take great joy in watching me shovel food into my mouth in a manner that did probably not make me look classy enough to be in this place.

"This is really good," I said in between bites.

"It is," he agreed, cutting into his chicken. He wasn't eating half as quickly as I was. In fact, he seemed to have something on his mind.

"Is everything okay?" I asked.

"Oh, yes. Everything's fine. No reason to worry." He smiled at me, but I wasn't convinced.

"Are you really fine with everything that's going on? I know it's a lot to take. And we still have so much to talk about."

"I am. And I know that. But I also know that I love you, and that we'll make it through whatever life throws our way just as long as we stick together. I know it's more than just alpha-omega instincts between us."

I tilted my head. "You know, sometimes I do worry that it's all hormones." He smelled *so* good tonight. Part of me just wanted to rub myself on him.

"Phone sex," he said, a twinkle in his eyes. "You couldn't smell me then, could you?"

"No, just the sound of your voice..." And that had been enough. I sighed. He was right; I was in deep.

"It's okay," Matt said, stroking my leg with his foot underneath the table in a way that made me hunger for more contact. "I feel the same way about you. And once we're done with the main course, I have a surprise for you."

"A surprise?" What could it be? I made myself eat faster, even though I hadn't thought that was possible.

When I was done, Matt took me to the outdoors area of the restaurant. It had a glass wall as well as ceiling so it wasn't *really* outside, but you could see the lights from the harbor in the distance and the night sky above you. One table was set with cake for us—all the others were empty.

"I've had them clear out the area," Matt said.

I didn't even want to think about what that must have cost. "I thought you wanted everybody to see us."

"True. But for some moments, privacy is nice. Come, sit." He pulled out a chair for me and I lowered myself into it.

"This is the surprise?" I asked. "It's beautiful here."

He smiled and shook his head. "This isn't the surprise. This is. Watch." He pointed up at the sky. I looked. At first, I didn't see anything, but then, the fireworks started up. My eyes grew wide.

"Did you—"

"Shhh. Just enjoy the moment."

I did. I enjoyed it immensely. The fireworks lit up the sky in red and yellow and orange sparkles and flowers and even hearts. And I couldn't help but think of that one time we'd stolen away together during the town's summer festival, when everyone was watching the fireworks and no one paid us any mind. We'd run to one of his family's yachts and watched the spectacle from there. I remembered wishing back then that I could just sail away with him.

I'd never have imagined it possible that I'd get my own private fireworks show from him one day.

"Oh, Matt. This is too much."

"Keep looking up," he said.

And the moment I looked back to the sky, I saw a question written among the stars. *The* question.

*Will you marry me?*

"Oh my God." My heart stopped still. I looked back at Matt—who'd gone down on one knee beside me, holding a small jewelry box in his hands. "What are you doing?" I asked. I *knew* of course. I just couldn't believe it. "Matt—"

He gave me a smile and put a finger on my lips. "I'm doing exactly what I should have been doing years ago. Just listen for a moment, okay?"

I nodded. Too astonished to do anything else.

He took a deep breath, and then he spoke. "I know I've already said that I love you, but I feel it can't be said enough. The years I've spent without you have been miserable. I never want to leave you again. I want to raise our children together. I want to wake up next to you every morning. I want you to be mine in every way that you can be mine, and I want to be yours. Elias Stevens, will you do me the honor of marrying me?"

I stared at Matt, heart beating a mile a minute. Did he really just ask me to marry him? In the stars and on his knee? "Of course I'll marry you!"

He let out a breath. "Oh thank God, I was getting really nervous for a second there."

I laughed, and then I leaned down and kissed him. He ran his hand into my hair and kissed me back, and I was sure that I was the happiest omega in all of Oceanport.

# Elias

The next few weeks were the best of my life. Matt was busy with his new job, yes, but he still spent as much time as he could over at my place. He told me this was a) because he wanted Jake to get used to his presence, and b) because he just couldn't get enough of me. He underlined the last point by kissing me every chance he got. Something else, he said, that people needed to get used to.

I did stop him from undressing me in our living room, though. Way too public as long as I was still living with my brother. But we were already talking about moving to a different place—together. We'd be staying in town, but we wanted a house that was ours. A place we could do whatever we liked... as long as the kids weren't around, anyway. But we also agreed that we couldn't start looking at places before we'd talked to Jake about everything.

Which we decided to do about a month after Matt proposed to me. I was almost at the end of my first trimester and we figured it was best to talk to him before he started asking why Daddy was getting so fat.

Together, we fetched him from school one day and took him out to a park where he could run around with Fiona and tire himself out a bit before we had our conversation. That had been Matt's idea, but it wasn't a bad one. He really understood energetic little alphas, and I loved seeing the two of them together. Especially when Jake asked Matt to race him and Fiona, and Matt just couldn't say no.

Both of them returned to me all red in the face after a few minutes. I laughed, and decided my kid had probably run enough.

I handed both of my boys a cookie when they sat on the bench with me while sneaking Fiona a treat. Funny enough, the old dog was the only one not breathing hard. "Good girl," I said, petting her. Then I turned to Jake, who'd hopped on the bench next to me, letting his feet dangle in the air. "Matt and I need to talk to you about something."

"Yeah?" He eyed Matt and me suspiciously while nibbling on his cookie. "Am I in trouble?"

I ruffled his hair. "You're not in trouble."

"Then what?" Fiona rested her head on Jake's knees and he put a piece of his cookie in her mouth, even though he knew he wasn't supposed to do that. But this once, I let it slide.

"You know how Matt and I are a couple?"

He tilted his head, as if wondering why I was asking such a stupid question. "Yeah."

"Well, we were thinking about making it

official." Matt grabbed my hand as I said this, while Jake continued to look at me curiously.

"But you already told everyone. You even kissed in front of my school." He made a face. I wasn't going to apologize, though. As his daddy, embarrassing him every now and then was part of my job.

Matt took over. "What your daddy is trying to say is that we'd like to get married."

"Oh." Jake's eyes widened. "Does that mean you'll get a huge cake like Tommy's mom did last year?"

"Yeah," I said. "There'll be cake."

"But will it be huge?"

I glanced at Matt. "I'm sure we can arrange that."

"Yay! When are you getting married?" Jake asked like he couldn't wait.

I licked my lips. "We haven't settled on a date yet, but we thought doing it in the summer might be nice." On top of giving us a little time because spring had only just started.

"Oh, then there should be ice cream too," Jake suggested. "Cause it'll be hot."

"Like you need it to be hot to want ice cream," I joked. "We just really wanted to talk to you about this because we'll also be moving together when we're married. All three of us. I want to make sure you're okay with that."

"Three?" He looked skeptical. "Does that mean Uncle Griff isn't coming with us?"

"No." I put an arm around Jake's shoulders.

"Uncle Griff needs to live alone for a while. But he'll come visit. And you can visit him anytime you want. We're not leaving town."

"Oh. Okay, then. He should get a piece of the cake, though."

"He will."

"Okay." Jake nodded once, apparently satisfied.

I inhaled. "There is... one more thing." I looked to Matt, who gave me a reassuring smile.

"There's more?" Jake asked.

"You're going to be a big brother," Matt said, before I could get another word in.

Jake seemed suspicious. "A big brother?"

"Yes, in a few months, you'll have a baby brother or a baby sister."

"Tommy got a baby sister." Jake grimaced. "He says babies are stupid and cry a lot."

Ugh. Part of me wanted to strangle Tommy for making this hard on me, but Matt took over the conversation before I could get too upset.

"Babies cry because they don't know better," he said. "They're these helpless little things that can't even talk. They can't really do much. They can't run like we just did. They can't even walk until they're almost a year old."

"Do they cry because they're so bored?" Jake asked.

"No, they cry because they need our help and our protection."

Finally I could see where Matt was going with this, trying to appeal to Jake's alpha instincts to get him on board. Pretty clever, actually. I wouldn't have thought of that, at least not so quickly. It was nice not being alone in figuring this stuff out.

"I can protect them," Jake said, puffing out his chest and totally taking the bait.

"I know." Matt nodded. "The baby will be lucky to have a strong big brother like you."

"I *am* strong." Jake beamed and jumped off the bench. "I can lift Fiona!"

I pulled him back by the arm. "But you won't." I couldn't let *everything* slide. "She's an old lady and you need to be gentle with her."

"Okay. But I could!"

"I'm sure you could." Matt stood up as well. "Race you again? First to the swing set!" And as soon as he'd spoken, he started running.

"Unfair!" Jake yelled, trying to catch up.

I stayed behind laughing, feeling in my bones that everything was going to be just fine somehow. Having another baby wasn't what I'd planned, and it put a stop to my dreams of returning to college, but I was used to life interfering with my plans. I wasn't going to feel bitter about it. What was the point?

* * *

Over the next few weeks, we tried hard to include Jake in everything that was going on. We took him to see the house we wanted to buy—which was gorgeous, two stories, huge backyard and just outside town. We let him help pick out some toys for the baby—and made sure to buy him one as well. We even took him along to a doctor's visit so he could see his new sibling on an ultrasound—which he actually found pretty exciting.

The only thing that bothered him was that we didn't want to find out the gender before birth, but we weren't going to budge on that. I wanted there to be an element of surprise.

In the first week of May, just around the time I was really starting to show, Matt announced our engagement in the local newspaper. It was a little bit embarrassing when I went grocery shopping that day and every other person stopped to congratulate me. Especially knowing that many of these people had been talking about me behind my back not too long ago. But Matt said I should be proud, and I tried to be, answering everyone with a smile before excusing myself to get on with my day.

I came home a little bit exhausted from my shopping trip, and Griff laughed at me as I huffed, putting the groceries away. "You try being pregnant and running errands!" I told him. "Actually I'm really looking forward to the day it'll be you in my place." I tossed him an apple and he caught it.

"Not for a long time!" he said. Then, "Is it really so bad?"

"Not the pregnancy so much." I wiped some sweat from my forehead. "But it's like everyone in town suddenly loves me. Super weird."

"Ah yeah. I saw your thing in the paper. I can't believe he took out a whole page. Must have cost him a fortune."

"I guess money doesn't really matter to you

when you have as much as he does." I lowered myself in a chair and let the rest of the groceries be for a moment.

"And I guess he must really want everyone to know that this baby is going to be legitimate."

*What?* I stared at Griff, mouth half-open. Was that really what this was? No, it couldn't be. Could it? How hadn't this thought occurred to me before?

Griff rubbed the back of his neck. "Did I say something wrong? I just figured that's what you guys wanted. I mean, you did get engaged the day after you found out you were pregnant."

"You know I don't care about legitimacy!"

He shrugged, the gesture almost apologetic. "I know *you* don't."

I cringed. Because what he was saying made sense, and I didn't *want* it to. This baby's legitimacy status was *not* why Matt had proposed to me. Was it?

Only one way to find out.

I grabbed my phone.

# Matthew

---◆---

Eli sounded upset when I answered the phone. "Is something the matter?" I asked, sitting in my dad's office. These days I spent so much time with Eli and Jake that I had to pour every other minute I had into work just to stay caught up.

"We need to meet." There was a certain urgency to Eli's tone that worried me.

"Did something happen? Is Jake alright?"

"Jake's fine, just meet me!"

"Okay." I glanced at the clock that hung on the wall above the door. It was still early evening. "Would you like to go eat something?"

"No, I'm not hungry. Just...Let's meet by the playground in the park, okay?"

"Okay," I said, really worried now that Eli didn't want food. So far, he'd been ravenous for this whole pregnancy.

Leaving the office and the mansion behind, I made my way to the town's park. The playground was mostly deserted, but Eli was already waiting for me when I got there. And he looked tense.

Absolutely beautiful with his belly getting round, but tense.

"Hey," I said, approaching.

He looked up at the sound of my voice. "Hey. Should we walk a bit? I think I need to walk."

"Yeah, sure. Let's." I took his hand and led him down the path, remembering that night we'd come here to talk. When he'd first told me about Jake all those months ago. Part of me still couldn't believe how much my life had changed since then.

"I saw the announcement in the paper," Eli started.

"Yeah? Did you like it?"

"It was... certainly eye-catching. You really wanted everyone to know about us, didn't you?" He laughed, but it sounded forced.

"Eli? What's wrong?"

He stopped walking and shook his head. "My brother just said something stupid. Like that you wanted everyone to know how this baby was going to be legitimate. Like that was why you proposed to me."

"Is that really what you think?" I squeezed his hand. "I love you, Eli. I thought you knew that."

"I do! But you have to agree the timing was pretty perfect. What with you proposing to me right after you found out about the baby."

"Okay." I took a deep breath. "I'm not going to deny that hearing about the baby made me want to marry you *even more*. But it was not the only reason I proposed. I spent a long time living in a loveless marriage. Trust me. I would never voluntarily do that again. The reason I want to marry you is because you make me smile, because when I'm with you I feel like everything fits, like everything is going to be all right and the world is beautiful. Because when I'm not with you I miss you so much it hurts. *That* is why I want to marry you." I gazed into Eli's eyes, willing him to believe me. He needed to know that I didn't want to marry him for one single reason but for a million of them.

Eli grabbed both of my hands and returned my gaze. There was such longing in his eyes, but he didn't seem entirely convinced yet. "So what you're saying is that it doesn't matter to you when we get married? If we're not getting married because of the baby the date should not matter, right?"

I bit my teeth together. He had me there. No, the baby wasn't the only reason I wanted to get married, but it was included in my reasons. Getting married before it was born would just make so many things so much easier. It would bring us a step closer to gaining the acceptance of my family. I knew that didn't matter to Eli, but it still mattered to me. But how could I tell him that now without him taking it the wrong way? I just had to try. "Of course we can get married whenever we want, but the sooner we do it the better. Don't you think so?"

"It really doesn't matter to me if we get married now or in a year. All that matters to me is that we're together."

"You're right." I freed one of my hands to run it through his soft hair. "We're always going to be together." I rested my forehead against his. "But don't you see that marrying sooner rather than later could make some things a bit easier?"

"You really are thinking about the baby's legitimacy, aren't you?" Eli took a step back. "I didn't want to believe that my brother's right, but this actually matters to you."

"Is that really such a bad thing? I want to show my family that I'm being serious. I want them to accept this baby, and I want them to accept Jake. What's wrong with that?"

Eli shook his head. "There's nothing wrong with that. I just don't think it's going to happen." He sighed. "A DNA test isn't going to help. A marriage isn't going to help. Your family loves to look down on people like me, and once you marry me, they'll look down on you too. That's all that's going to happen. I wish it was different, but it isn't. And it scares me that you still can't see that. If you want to please your family, you can't marry me."

We hadn't talked about the incident involving Jake and my mother since the day it had happened, but it seemed like it was still on Eli's mind. Why else would he get so upset? "You don't know that nothing is going to help until we try. I'm not going to let them talk to Jake like that again. I promise. You just have to give me a chance to make it work."

"And what if it never works?" Eli burst out. "Will you still be happy then? If you can't fulfill your family's expectations? If they never accept Jake? Or the baby I'm carrying right now?"

"That's not—"

"Don't tell me it's not going to happen,

because there's a very real possibility that it will. And I honestly don't know what you'll do then. That's the problem here."

"I'll—"

"No," Eli cut me off. He looked like he was about to cry and the sight tore at my heartstrings. "Don't tell me now. Please. Think about it." He took a deep breath. "Do you know I got a letter in the mail this morning?"

"A letter?" That was a sudden change of topic.

"Yeah." He sniffed. "A reply to the college application I sent out. They accepted me." He said it with a smile, even though his voice sounded sad. "I'm not going to go, because I have to put my kids first. That's what it means to be a good omega. To be a good parent. I have my priorities. And you really need to think about yours."

His news left me speechless. I so wanted him to go. He was smart, he'd worked hard, and he deserved it.

But life didn't always work like that, did it?

Eli stepped up to me and placed a kiss on my lips, then he withdrew again far too quickly, before I could close my arms around him. "Please think about it all," he said.

And then he walked away from me.

* * *

I returned home with a heavy heart. *Think*, he'd said. I *had* thought about it all. I was going to marry the man I loved and then we were going to raise our children together and live happily ever after. That was the general plan.

Maybe Eli was right, and it wasn't detailed enough. I had no idea how my family fit into my plans. I wanted to keep all doors open for my kids, but Eli seemed to think that plan was doomed from the start.

I rubbed my face, walking up the stairs, until I heard my mother's shrieking voice behind me. "Matthew Joseph Lowell!" she shouted.

Full name? Great, somebody else who wasn't happy with me today. Trying hard not to sigh, I turned around to her. "Mother?" At least she had started talking regularly again.

"You come down here right this second and tell me what that... that *thing* in the newspaper was about!"

So she'd read the paper. Lovely. She'd never done that while Father was alive. And it wasn't that I wanted to *hide* my engagement from her, but this wasn't necessarily the way I'd planned for to find out about it. "Elias Stevens and I got engaged," I told her as calmly as I could.

"You can't get engaged! You haven't even met all the ladies I wanted to introduce you to yet! You're being foolish and you don't know what you're missing out on!" She gestured wildly with her arms to underline just how preposterous she thought all of this was.

"No, it's fine, Mother. I've made my decision, and you need to accept it." *Please just accept it.* I couldn't take all this fighting anymore. My family had never been super harmonious, but these last few months had been rough.

"You expect me to accept this?" She scoffed. "You're my son, and I'm not going to watch you ruin your life."

"I can make my own decisions."

She laughed, as if the very idea was ridiculous. Of course it was, to her. She'd been running the show my whole life.

And suddenly I wondered whether that was the kind of parent *I* was going to be—just for trying to get my kids into this business. I wanted to do what was best for them... but my mother had often used the same line of reasoning with me.

*You won't find a better bride than Danielle.*

*You have to major in business if you want to be successful in life.*

*You won't be happy if you don't marry.*

"You know what, Mother?" I said. "Elias is pregnant with another child from me. You're going to have another grandchild."

She narrowed her eyes. "Another bastard?"

"Not if we get married," I said, just to test her.

She bristled. "You can't marry that omega!"

"And I can't make you happy, either, can I?" I sighed, because as much as I didn't want to admit it to myself, I knew that Eli was right. My family would never welcome him or our children, no matter what I did.

"You could *try*," my mother insisted. "And to think that your father and I had such high hopes for you!"

Hopes or expectations? I knew all about the

expectations that I tried to live up to.

And what for?

To please my parents?

To fulfill my duty as the alpha of this family?

Frederica was right. I was far too obsessed with those things.

I shook my head to myself. It was time to think beyond what it meant to be a good alpha. What I needed to be now was a good parent. *And* a good fiancé.

# Elias

I wasn't sure what to expect when Matt called me during my lunch break the next day. Honestly, I was a bit apprehensive to answer the call, but he sounded happy.

"Are you at the shelter right now?" he asked.

"I am, why?"

"Because I'm in the parking lot. Come out and meet me, please."

"Okay," I said slowly. What was that about?

When I got to the parking lot, I spotted Matt, wearing a heavy-looking rucksack on his back and carrying a basket in his hand.

"Care to have lunch with me?" he asked, lifting the basket up.

"You packed a picnic? I only have half an hour."

"That's enough," he said, glancing at the forest bordering the shelter. "C'mon. I got takeout from your favorite burger joint."

"Andrew's?" I asked, saliva gathering in my mouth. Andrew's had the best burgers *ever*.

"Not like there's another burger joint in town," Matt said with a smile. "So will you join me?" He held his free hand out to me.

"Can't say no when you're being this romantic." I chuckled, and let him lead me a short way into the woods. As it turned out, he'd packed a blanket in his rucksack, and now he spread it out on a patch of grass for us to sit. "You really thought this through," I noted.

"Yeah." He sat. "Not the only thing I've thought about either."

He handed me a burger and I sat with him. And I couldn't resist holding the burger up to my nose and breathing in the smell. Oh God so good.

"Do I need to get jealous of that burger?" Matt joked.

"Sorry, still ravenous." I tore the wrapping off my food and took a large bite. "I'm going to get so fat."

"You look perfect." Matt kissed the side of my forehead. "Really, you've never looked better."

"I'm going to get bigger."

"I'm looking forward to it." He kissed my lips and I let out a little sigh. Why couldn't things always be this easy? But he'd said he'd thought about things so maybe...

"Was there something you needed to tell me?" I asked. "Is that why you came?" I just hoped he wasn't trying to prepare me for some bad news with the good food.

"Actually, I have something for you." He reached for his Rucksack again.

"Did you hide more burgers in there?"

"Not more burgers, I'm afraid. But I thought you might like this too." He spread a bunch of thick books out on the blanket in front of me. On closer inspection, they were all medical books.

"What..."

"I called up the college and asked them what books you were going to need."

"The college?" What was he talking about? "But I'm not going. I told you that." And yet I couldn't stop myself from reaching for one of the books and paging through it. *Ah, the smell of new books.*

So much knowledge between these pages. Knowledge that could help me realize my dream, if only... I sighed.

"I want you to go," Matt said, face serious.

"I won't have time when the baby comes." I put the book down again.

"Yeah, you will."

"I thought I'd told you I don't want a full-time nanny."

"And we're not going to hire one." He grabbed my hands. "I'll do it."

I blinked. "You'll what?" Was I dreaming all of this?

"I'll take care of the baby while you're studying."

"But you have your job." I was tempted to touch his forehead and see if he was running a fever or something. Where was this coming from?

His lips curled up in a grin so wide it rivaled

the Cheshire Cat's. "I quit."

"You what?" My eyes must have been as wide as saucers. Matt quitting his job?

He shrugged. "You were right, my family sucks. I've thought about my priorities. I've missed so much with Jake, I don't want to miss a second of this little one." He inched closer to me and gently put a hand on my belly. "I don't want to be like my parents," he said, catching my eyes. "I don't want the kids to remember me as this dude who spent the whole day in his office and never had time for anything."

"But you're an alpha. How is staying home with the kids going to make you happy?"

"I'm more than just an alpha, the same way you're more than just an omega. Don't you think it's time we broke the stereotypes?"

I huffed. "You know I've tried that before." Everything I always wanted seemed to be right in front of me, suddenly, but I was still afraid to reach out and take it.

"So you'll try again." Matt rested his forehead on mine. "We'll try together. And we'll make it. I know it."

"And our kids can be whatever they want?"

"Whatever they want. Everyone deserves a chance to follow their dreams. And that includes you." Matt chuckled, and then he kissed me. I kissed him back and thanked my lucky stars for whatever had made him change his mind.

I was going to go back to college! I was marrying Matt! Without marrying his family!

It all seemed too good to be true, even knowing that it was. Closing my eyes, I tried to carve this moment into my memories. Whenever Matt and I were facing hard times in the future, I wanted to remember how I'd felt this day. To remember that we could make it through anything.

And then, because I was still pregnant and starving, I broke the kiss to get another bite of my burger.

"You sure I shouldn't be jealous of that thing?" Matt asked, laughing.

"All this excitement has made me hungry!"

"Everything makes you hungry these days."

"True." I took another bite and licked my fingers. Yum, ketchup. "It's hard work making a baby."

"Yeah?" Matt shot me a filthy grin. "I seem to remember you enjoying it quite a bit."

"Well, yeah, the beginning is fun," I admitted. "Then comes the hard part. And then the even harder part."

"What's the even harder part?"

"The birth." I sighed. "Jake took me *hours*."

Matt wrapped his arm around my shoulders. "But this time I'll be there with you."

"Yeah." I leaned into him and reached up to hold his hand. "Will we be married by then?"

"Up to you," he said. "It doesn't matter to me whether we get married before or after the birth, but I am making you mine." He dipped his head to kiss my neck, making a shudder go down my spine.

I put the burger aside and kissed his head. "I'm yours already."

Now and forever.

\* \* \*

"You don't mind that I'm going to move out, do you?" I asked my brother one evening early in June when the days were getting warmer and it was nice to sit on the front steps of the house.

"I'll be fine," Griff said. "I'm sure you'll still cart the kids over here when you need a babysitter."

I gave him a sheepish smile, because he *was* babysitting for me again that night. I called on him a lot these days. Something about my pregnancy seemed to give Matt a really high sex drive and we both knew we had to make use of that now before the baby was here—which we did. I could still feel some soreness in my ass from the night before. It was a good kind of soreness, though, reminding me of a night wonderfully spent in the embrace of my lover. Ever since I'd started showing, Matt liked to take things slow in the bedroom, placing kisses all over me, but especially my belly, before he went down to business. Some nights it was torture to wait that long, but I really couldn't complain about how thorough he was being. He certainly never left me unsatisfied.

But I wasn't going to tell my brother all of that.

"I can promise you you'll see enough of my kids," I told him instead, trying to be casual. "Jake loves you, and I'm sure the new one will too. Besides, you'll finally have some time to work on your own love life."

Griff scoffed. "Like there's anything there to work on."

"Oh, don't be that way. What about your mysterious cupcake supplier?" I hadn't forgotten about that.

Griff looked aside, but not before I could see his cheeks color. "I only taste-test for him."

I had to keep my laughter inside, because I didn't want to ridicule my brother, but his crush was so obvious. I couldn't wait to see where this was going. "Well, let me know if it ever turns into more."

Griff didn't say anything, but I didn't give him much time either, because Matt's car was pulling up in front of the house, and I had some news to share with him. Two pieces of news, actually.

I ran up to my handsome alpha as he stepped out of the car and kissed him. Doing this in public still felt strange, but also amazing.

"You seem in a good mood today," Matt commented.

"I am." I grinned. "I just handed in my notice at work. You should have seen the look on that stupid Harold's face."

Matt's face lit up. "Really? That's great! I'm so happy for you!"

"Thanks for making it possible." I gave him another kiss.

"Please, you deserve to go back to school."

"But I couldn't do it if you hadn't quit your job. And I know your job was important to you."

He shook his head. "It was just a job, and I'm

actually much happier keeping contact to my mother and my sister to a minimum."

"How are they doing?" I asked, more out of courtesy than anything.

He shrugged. "Alright, I guess. My sister still screams at me over the phone once a week, but she'll get over it. I really don't want to think about it too much."

"Well, I have the perfect thing to take your mind off your family."

"You are my family."

"I know." I couldn't help but smile at his words. We weren't married yet, but I was definitely his—and very happy that way. "But that's not what I meant." I took his hand and laid it on my belly. He looked at me curiously. "The baby's been kicking today. And I'm hoping..." *Come on, baby.* I wanted to share this moment with Matt, the way I hadn't gotten to with my first pregnancy. And then it happened. The baby kicked, and Matt's eyebrows shot up. I felt a grin break out on my face. "You felt it?"

"I did! Wow! You really have a baby in there!"

Laughter bubbled out of me, because he sounded so incredulous. "You didn't believe it before?"

"No, I did! It's just... different feeling it."

"Good different?"

"Amazing different." Wrapping his arms around me, he pulled me in for a deep kiss that made my head spin in all the good ways. "I can't wait to meet this little one," he said.

I gave him a grin. "Oh, you will. And then you might regret your decision to be a full-time dad when you sit atop a mountain of diapers."

He snorted. "I will never regret this decision."

I simply pressed my lips to his because I felt much the same way. I'd made a lot of stupid decisions in my life, but giving us another shot was definitely not one of them.

# Matthew

About three weeks before Eli's due date, I took Jake on a trip to the big city to have some one-on-one time with him before the baby arrived. He was getting excited about being a big brother soon, but I wanted to make sure he knew how important he was to me and his daddy even with the new sibling on the way.

We spent half a day at the museum. They had a special exhibit on dinosaurs there, and Jake got a real kick out of looking at the huge skeletons. I handed him my cell phone in camera mode and let him go wild taking pictures. It was cute to watch, really.

Until the cell phone rang and put an abrupt end to our trip.

"It's Uncle Griff. He wants to talk to you," Jake said, handing me the phone. "He sounds scary."

Scary? I held the phone to my ear. "What's up, Griff?"

Eli's in labor," Griff screeched. "I'm taking him to the hospital. You gotta get here."

*Oh for the love of...* The one day I'd left town!

"I'll be there as fast as I can." I ended the call, took Jake by the hand, and hurried out of the museum.

"Where are we going?" Jake asked, rightfully confused. "I haven't seen all the dinosaurs!"

"I'm sorry, but we need to get to the hospital."

Jake tugged on my arm. "But you promised I could get something from the gift shop!"

"We really don't have the time. The baby is coming."

"The baby?" Jake made big eyes.

"Yes, you're going to be a big brother today."

"Cool!"

I smiled. "Do you see now why we have to hurry?"

"I'll be quick!" And with that said, he dragged me in the direction of the gift shop. I groaned. As much as I was looking forward to the baby, it had the worst timing! And wasn't it too early anyway? The doctor had said it would be another three weeks.

Should I be worried?

I bit my lower lip while Jake ran to one of the shelves and grabbed a red dinosaur plushie from it. "I want this one!"

"Fine." I paid for it. At least he'd decided quickly.

Jake grabbed the plushie back from the lady working the register once I'd paid and took my

276

hand. "C'mon, we have to hurry."

I almost laughed. Almost. But he was right; we did have to get back to Oceanport quickly. Griff had sounded as if the baby would be there any second, and I didn't want to miss the birth for anything. I knew that Eli had been in labor for a long time with Jake, but the second time was supposed to be faster, right?

In normal traffic conditions, it took nearly two hours from here to Oceanport. In *normal* traffic. But that day, traffic sucked. Of course it did.

It was all I could do not to start cursing every other driver while I had my son in the car with me.

"Can't you go faster?" he asked.

But no, I could not. It seemed everybody wanted to get out of the city.

I let Jake sound the horn, though. Not that it did anything.

All in all, it took us the better part of an hour just to get out of the city, and then we still had to get back to town. It was around this time that I started getting agitated phone calls about what was taking me so long.

"I'm doing the best I can," I told Eli on the cell.

"Yeah? So am I, but this baby isn't going to wait forever so you better get your ass here."

I grimaced. "Just so you know, I put you on speaker and Jake's in the car."

"Hi, Daddy!"

Eli groaned, but switched to a friendlier tone of voice. "Hey, kiddo. Tell Matt to hurry up, okay?"

"I will!"

"Good! See you soon." Eli ended the call, and I stepped on the gas a little harder.

We made good time too, until Jake decided he really, really needed to *go*. And no, it could not wait.

*Oh, the joys of being a parent.*

Swallowing down some curse words, I stopped by the side of the road where I spotted some trees that would obscure us from sight.

"But there's no toilet here," Jake complained.

"That's okay, buddy, just try to aim for that flower." I pointed at some weed with yellow blossoms.

"Can I really?" He shifted his weight rapidly from one foot to the other.

"Of course you can." *And please don't pee yourself.*

I looked aside as he pulled his pants down and went to business. Of course my phone chose that moment to ring again.

"Hello?"

Eli's voice greeted me, sounding even more irritated than before. "You're still not here! You promised you were going to be here!"

"Jake needed to water some flowers."

"Don't tell Daddy!" Jake shouted.

"What was that?" Eli asked.

"Nothing. Listen, I'll be there in twenty minutes!"

"You better be! They want me to push this thing out already. And honestly, I'm tempted!"

"Right. I'll get back in the car." And I did, just as soon as Jake had zipped his pants back up.

It took me another half hour to get us to the hospital, and once I'd parked the car, I grabbed my kid, who was still carrying that stupid plushie, and sprinted inside. I was *not* going to miss this birth. I'd missed too much of my time as a parent already. Yeah, being a parent could be tiring some days, but I loved being there for my son, and I wanted to be there for this child too—from the moment it came into this world.

And I was going to make it, *damn it*.

Nothing was going to slow me down.

Until something did.

"Dad!" Jake yelled, trying to get my attention.

I stopped immediately. "What?"

"They have flowers!" He pointed to another damn gift shop while all I could think about was what he'd just called me. "We need to bring Daddy flowers."

"Okay." Like in trance, I set Jake down and walked over to the gift shop with him, where I quickly grabbed a bouquet of their prettiest flowers and paid for it. Then I gave them to Jake to carry. And I decided not to comment on the fact that he'd just called me Dad for the first time. I didn't want to make him feel awkward about it.

But I *was* pretty damn happy.

I was still grinning when we finally made it to the delivery room. Griff was standing in front of the door, waiting for us. I left Jake with him and hurried inside.

"Oh God, you're finally here!" Eli was red in the face, already pushing. "Come here!"

I ignored the doctor and the nurse in the room and went to stand by Eli's bed. He grabbed my hand and squeezed so hard I thought he might just break it. But I was so relieved that I'd gotten here in time that I didn't mind. "Thanks for waiting."

"I wasn't waiting! I'm hard at work!"

"And almost done here too," the doctor chimed in. "The baby's crowning."

Wow. Sounded like I really *had* gotten here just in time.

"Keep pushing!" the doctor said.

Eli looked like he wanted to throw some profanities at him, but instead he let out a sound that was very nearly a scream. And then soon after I heard a different cry.

The first cry of my newborn child.

And it took my breath away.

"It's a girl!" the doctor pronounced, holding her up.

"Wow." It was all I could think to say while Eli let himself fall back on the bed, clearly exhausted but with a smile on his face.

"We have a little girl," he muttered.

"Yeah, we do." I leaned down to give him a quick kiss. "You did so well."

"Would you like to cut the umbilical cord?" the doctor addressed me.

"Of course." I took the scissors from him and made a clean cut. Then the nurse took my little girl away to get her wrapped up.

"Have you decided on a name?" Eli asked.

Since I hadn't been given a say in Jake's name, Eli had said that I could pick this time. It was a generous offer, and I was a little nervous to screw it up, but once the nurse laid the baby on Eli's chest and I got another look at her beautiful face, I knew I'd made the right choice. "Olivia," I said.

Eli's lips curled up as he stroked our daughter's cheek with one finger. "Welcome to the world, Olivia."

"You're okay with the name?"

"I love it."

"I'm glad. I love it too. And you. And her." *So much.* I'd been a little worried about becoming a full-time parent, but once Eli handed Olivia to me, all my fears vanished into a puff of smoke. Natural child rearing instincts or not, alpha or omega, it didn't matter. This was my family now, and I'd made the right decisions.

\* \* \*

"Where's the baby?" Jake asked, bouncing into the room alongside Griff as soon as Eli and the baby had recovered a little bit.

"Come here," Eli said, waving the boy toward him while still holding Olivia.

"I brought presents!" Jake said proudly. "For the baby and for you!" He held up the plushie and the flowers. I'd no idea he'd wanted to give the dinosaur to his new sister, but now I was glad we'd stopped at the gift shop.

"Thank you," Eli said with a smile. "The flower are lovely, and I'm sure your sister is going to love her new toy."

"It's a girl?" Jake peeked at the bundle in Eli's arms while I took the flowers from him and put them into a glass with water.

"She's beautiful," Griff said. "So cute."

I grinned to myself. She totally was.

"We're going to have so much fun!" Jake announced, and the level of glee in his voice promised me a world of trouble and shenanigans. But that was okay. I loved my mate, and I loved my children, and no amount of schoolboy mischief or toddler tantrums could keep me away from them anymore.

This was all so different from everything I'd ever imagined—and everything my parents had ever wanted for me. And yet, I felt like this was the best day of my life. And I couldn't wait for the rest of it.

# Epilogue

ELIAS

---

*E*ight months later

Thirty minutes before the wedding ceremony, Jake came bursting into the dressing room where I was checking my white suit in front of the mirror. "Daddy!"

"What's up?"

"Dad asks if you're ready yet."

I tried to straighten my hair a bit, but it was no use. "Almost."

"You look funny in that suit," Jake said.

I chuckled. He was right. I did look a bit different from usual, but it was customary for omegas to marry in white. I didn't care about the tradition so much, but Matt said he liked the color on me, and after I'd made him wait *this long* to get married... he could totally have me whichever way he wanted me.

"Do you have the rings?" I asked Jake.

"Of course I do!" He puffed his chest out, ever so proud that we were trusting him with this task. And he was *so* cute in his navy suit, trying to look important.

"Good." I went down on one knee to hug him. "Now remember what I told you."

"I know! Walk slowly with the rings to the altar. No running. No jumping."

"Good boy." I kissed his hair and let him go. He was getting so big now. I couldn't believe he was eight already, soon to be nine.

Which meant this wedding was nearly ten years overdue.

When it was time for me to walk down the aisle, my brother walked with me, giving me away in place of the parent I hadn't spoken to in forever. But it seemed only fitting that Griff should be here with me. I owed so much to him. I couldn't wait for the day I got to return the favor.

"Good luck," Griff whispered as he let me go.

But who needed luck when he had the most handsome man waiting for him at the altar?

Matt's whole face lit up as he met my eyes. "You look stunning."

"So do you." I gave the compliment back with a smile. Matt was wearing black today, and I'm sure we contrasted nicely. The wedding pictures would be beautiful. Actually, everything looked great.

Matt had rented the town hall for this wedding, and Griff had been in charge of the decor. He had a real hand for it, using bright flowers and pastel colors to transform the hall into something that looked straight out of a fairy tale. *Only the best for my brother,* he'd said, even though he wasn't the one paying for this.

Not that money was an issue when you were marrying the richest man in town. Matt might have quit his job, but he still had so much in savings and investments that we weren't going to be scrounging for money anytime soon. Still, we'd kept expenses relatively low. We had no one to impress. Matt's family hadn't shown up, only some colleagues and old friends—and Frederica, who'd insisted on sitting in the front.

And *my* guests... Well, there was a row of people with cats and dogs from the shelter that made me smile when my eyes wandered their way. Fiona was there too, of course, sitting with some of the friends I'd made at college.

It was perfect. It was more than I'd ever dreamed of.

After all the gossip I'd had to endure, who'd have thought that someone was ever going to make an honest omega out of me? And all while I went back to college and left the child rearing to my mate!

"Ready to get this show started?" Matt asked with a small smile.

"You bet."

We turned to the officiator.

"We are gathered here today to celebrate the union between an alpha and an omega, to support and love one another in the way only true mates can. But today is not about duties or obligations or fulfilling your role in society. Today is about love, for nothing is more powerful than a bond forged by love. The love they hold for one another as well as the love they show their children every day. It is this love that will carry them through the trials and tribulations of life, and nothing brings me greater honor than joining these two in marriage today. Now let us hear their vows."

I looked at Matt, taking a deep breath because everything about this ceremony was making me teary. I wasn't going to cry, though. At least not until we'd exchanged rings! "Matt," I started, fiddling with the piece of paper in my hand. I'd written down so many words to say to him, but now I felt none of them were quite enough for what I wanted to express. "You have no idea how much I love you," I said, before my silence grew even longer. "And I don't have the words to tell you. Growing up, I always had this perfect vision of what my life was going to be like. I was going to be a vet and I was going to show everyone that omegas could be more than parents, and then you came and threw such a wrench into my plan." I had to laugh and he smiled as well. "It's because of you that I became a parent, but I also became so much more than that. You showed me that it's not important what society expects of me as long as I love what

I'm doing and I love who I'm with. The only thing I want to prove anymore is my love to you, and I'm going to keep doing that until the day that I die."

When I finished, Matt actually looked like his eyes were a little wetter than usual too! I grinned at him. Go me, nearly making an alpha cry.

Following my example, Matt didn't bother looking at his notes either. "You know that I've always had everything money could buy. People told me that I was lucky, that I should be happy, but I was only ever really happy when I was with you. I'm a fool, though, and it took me too long to see that. But people are right, and I really am lucky, because we got a second chance. I'm not going to waste it. I'm going to treasure you forever, because I have no treasure greater than you. You're the bearer of my children and the love of my life, and I promise to never leave your side again."

*Deep breath, Eli, not the time for tears yet.*

"Who has the rings?" the officiator asked.

"Here!" Jake walked up to us with a super-serious expression on his face. He held up a small black cushion with both rings placed on it. We'd opted for simple rings, because neither of us had wanted them to get stuck on anything, but they had our names engraved on the inside, and I loved them.

The officiator spoke again. "Do you, Matthew Lowell, take Elias Stevens to be your lawfully wedded husband?"

Matt met my eyes with a smile. "I do."

The officiator turned to me. "And do you Elias

Stevens take Matthew Lowell to be your lawfully wedded husband?"

It was a no-brainer. "I do."

"If there be anyone present who may show just and lawful cause why this couple may not be legally wed, let him speak now or forever hold his peace."

A second of silence, another.

I smiled at Matt. Nobody could stop us from being married.

"Exchange the rings."

We did.

"By the authority vested in me by the State of Maine, I hereby pronounce you husband and husband. You may now kiss."

Matt leaned in and pressed his lips to mine the moment the officiator stopped speaking. This was it. We were married. From somewhere, I heard barking. Fiona, in the front row. I hoped she was happy now, after getting us together all those years ago. She barked again. And then all the other dogs joined in until the hall was filled with the noise of excited animals.

Hell, even my kid joined the barking after a moment. People were going to be talking about this for *days*.

I didn't care, though. I simply laughed and leaned into my husband.

Let them talk.

I couldn't have asked for a better start into my new life.

# THE END

# About The Author

Ann-Katrin loves to write, read and dream. In her spare time, you can often catch her hunting wild plot bunnies in the fields of her imagination. In her other life, she's a mother and a translator, but writing about men and the men they fall in love with is so much more fun!

# Like this story?

Want to be updated whenever a new one comes out?

Sign up for Ann-Katrin's mailing list for sneak previews, cover reveals, and bonus content!

Sign up at *http://eepurl.com/bVJCqT*

And get two free bonus shorts—A Dragon's Christmas, and a Mercy Hills Valentine's!

# Other Books by Ann-Katrin

## <u>Mercy Hills Pack</u>
Mating the Omega (Book One)
Abel's Omega (Book Two)
Duke's Baby Deal (Book Three)
The Omega's Alpha (Book Four)

### *<u>Still to Come:</u>*
Legally Mated (Book Five)

## <u>Fires of Fate</u>
Under the Dragon's Spell (Book One)
The Dragon of His Dreams (Book Two)
Dragon's Love Song (Book Three)
Dragon's Miracle (Book Four)

## <u>Oceanport Omegas</u>
The Omega's Secret Baby (Book One)

Made in the USA
Coppell, TX
08 September 2021

62018717R00173